THE

A story about

NOTHING

making amends

MAN

Alfred Marc von Wellsheim

Dedication and thank you to

Madison, Mac, and Hayden.
To my beautiful offspring, you all opened my heart and creativity wide open. I love you. You are my everything.

To Susan Hamlett Spruill
Who knows a good story when she sees one. You were a driving force behind this tale.
Thank you for a lifetime of friendship and inspiration.

To Tiffany Herzog
I told you and that secret is between us.

To the readers.
Writing is the closest thing I have to a real home. It is exhilarating and tormenting taking a new idea and graduating it into a story. Shepherding down the creative river wondering if you will laugh, embrace, or hate it. My confession is that I love you all for taking the ride with my imagination.

Chapter 1

Cue the U2 song, "Beautiful Day."

Flashes of red and yellow streaks were all he could see in his mind's eye. He was becoming minimally conscious. His brain was cloudy, uncomfortable, and struggling to thread his thoughts together. He tried to lift himself up, but his body felt held down in place by a massive weight. His first thought was paralysis, but before he could panic, a wave of tranquility swept over him. It was a peace that surpassed his understanding and felt like a strong sensation, bringing him comfort.

Every fiber of his being was out of his control, and calmness made no sense. Gradually he could open his eyes ever so slightly. The light would hit his retina with a violent force, causing him to squeeze his eyelids shut. It occurred to him that he must have been in the dark for a lengthy period, but why? He started to remember colors such as blue, gold, and green, although his thoughts, mind, and soul were still saturated with the two primary colors. The other colors seemed to ignite his memory, introduce deeper thoughts, and bring him to profound consciousness. He worked on coming out of these red and yellow shades for what felt like hours, opening his eyes so slight that no passerby would have noticed his gradual awakening. He felt his heart and mind flourishing.

Slowly he started to connect to his senses. He could hear subtle noises. Wherever he was, the sounds were arousing him. If it were voices he heard, they were too faint to make out any dialogue. Slowly and steadily, a sound grew ever-present...a sound so captivating that he forgot about trying to see and focused on listening. The stirring indicated he was not alone; there was a presence near, but what or who? He felt the company of grace and love in his confusion.

Yet again, any compulsion he had to become anxious or even afraid was extinguished by that immense peace. It felt so unnatural that he was almost annoyed. But the annoyance gave way to his voice of reason. He realized that he was trying to rationalize his thoughts and feelings. An awakening was not about to obey the rules this man was trying to give it. He was becoming aware of his awareness. Still, he was not permitted to visit with his own thought life for long. It was a voice. The voice was singing. He found himself amused, pleased, and again easy consoled.

"Now a man gets crazy when his life is all gone ~ and a heart gets weary when it doesn't belong ~ when the road gets rocky Lord you've got to keep onnnnnnn ~ Let the new life come shining on through," the voice sang. It was an older gospel song, "Change in my Life." He lay aside his thoughts, reasoning, and questions to enjoy the singing. He reveled in the southern gospel song sung ever so softly, but he could make out every word. Again, it was that inconvenient and misplaced peace.

Jackson Riggs did not know his own name. He had no idea that he should have been placed in a nursing home or possibly hospice by now. He had been in a coma for seven weeks because of a car accident. Yet, his employer Barry Jenkins had decided to keep the patient in room 777 on the seventh floor of Orlando Health. His expenses were paid in full, and Barry would get reports on Riggs' condition daily. Jenkins is a man of wealth and influence that values Riggs' special services, loyalty, and discretion. Everything about Jenkins takes place on his own terms, and when you deal with him, you enter his world. He is a law unto himself, and people are easily intimidated by the man and his reputation. He relied heavily on Riggs to help with immediate problems. Both men were incredibly intense and forced to be reckoned with. Having Riggs on his side, Jenkins was free to focus his attention on what really mattered...money and more importantly, power. Now Jenkins was worried he would never be able to replace Riggs. All reports had remained grim for the titan of North Carolina. Doctors and specialists had long lost hope for Riggs. This was evident every time he scored a three on the Glasgow Coma Scale. He simply had no visible or determinable motor skills. Three is the lowest score a patient can get.

As Rosemary Appleman sang, she paid little attention to the patient's vegetative state. Her back was to Jackson when his eyes peeked open for the first time. She was preoccupied changing the IV bags that fed him. The feeding tube supplied him with all the nutrients, electrolytes, and medicines necessary to keep his body healthy. This prevented him from starving or dehydrating. Jackson was flat on his back, but he had become cognizant. "Why am I here, Rosemary?" Jackson asked, his voice raspy and direct but just above a whisper. "More importantly, who am I?" he continued.
Rosemary was startled, screamed, and fell back, but luckily into a wall. Her eyes were as big as saucers. Jackson looked at her, confused and alarmed as well. As their eyes met, Rosemary relaxed. "You, you, you are awake!" she spoke, dismayed. He just looked at her with a confused stare. She reached out and took his hand as she regained her footing from the wall. Rosemary moved in slow motion. Their eyes met. In the brief silence, without another word, they understood every thought each other

had. Immediately, Jackson Riggs knew Rosemary was genuinely a good person. A woman incredibly sensitive to everyone and everything. When Jackson gently squeezed her hand, excited goosebumps came over her. She knew nothing about this man but felt she was in the presence of goodness, possibly an angel. Rosemary studied him as if he were an alien. She was in awe. Her hand ran over his matted hair, then against his face and beard. Her touch made him feel alive.

"You are going to be just fine." She spoke without a hint of hesitation.

"I know," he replied with an eerie confidence. Rosemary noticed he wasn't arrogant. He hardly worried about his condition and as a result, she felt his peace and pulled her hand away.

"I am going to go get your doctor!" Rosemary exclaimed as she walked out of the hospital room. She walked with a slight limp but with a purpose.

Susan was busy at the nurse's station when Rosemary came rushing. However, Rosemary could have cared less.

"Get Doctor Selle right away! The patient in room 777 just woke up!" Susan stalled as if she had misheard, but when she focused, she saw Rosemary was very animated as she breathed heavily. Her expression was so clear and true that it was changing the atmosphere. Susan texted the doctor right away and then she paged him.

"He is awake?" Susan's face was stoic and full of doubt.

"Yes, and he spoke to me."

She was used to Rosemary's passion and devotion to ideas of faith, but this was as farfetched as any notion could be. Susan's eyes looked around. Her human psyche could not wrap her mind around what was happening. Surely Rosemary could not be right, but this was a hospital and patients tended to surprise the staff, just nothing this radical. Rosemary saw Susan's doubt and smiled, "Don't judge me just yet. At least not until you walk that country mile down to room 777." Susan relaxed her face and shifted gears. "Now stop waiting on Dr. Selle. At this point you're just stalling," Rosemary's smile was as innocent as that of a child. Susan made a few clicks on her computer before coming out from behind the help desk. She noticed that Rosemary didn't have her nametag. Susan was known for her attention to detail; nothing ever missed her observation.

"You forgot your name badge again." Rosemary was always the hospital's imperfect perfectionist. She was as much their big momma as their caregiver…always going the extra mile with patients. She was often known to take flowers left behind from a discharged patient to the elderly who did not have any. However, she was absent-minded regarding some of the details in her job that didn't involve caregiving. Her nametag had undoubtedly spent many shifts left in the car or at home despite having several. Suddenly Rosemary's expression changed, and she froze. Slowly she placed her hand where her nametag belonged as if placing her hand on her heart.

"Are you ok?" Susan asked, noticing her change in demeanor. She felt a rush of guilt. Susan wasn't trying to shame Rosemary.

"He," she paused, "said my name. How would he know my name?" she asked quietly.

Walking to room 777, Susan glanced out of a vast picture window. It was a clear day. The sky was a perfect shade of blue and the wind blew in the trees just enough to appear as though they were dancing. She wondered if all the world had come alive today to meet this mysterious man. One thing was certain Susan thought, *this is a beautiful day.*

Cue the Jackson Brown song, "Doctor My Eyes."

CHAPTER 2

Tiffany had just changed into her jeans and wife-beater tank top. Her long sandy blonde hair was down, and the day was finally nearing its end. She pulled her hair out of her face and into a ponytail. It was almost seven o'clock, time for her to relax while watching reruns of The Big Bang Theory. The house phone rang, a quick reminder of yet another thing she hated about her ex-husband. He had insisted they keep a landline, although everyone in the family had their own cell phone. Calls to the house phone were always spam. Occasionally, Jackson would make a call and almost speak in code. She was accustomed to Jackson being surrounded in secrecy and had long given up trying to decipher his conversations. The phone continued to ring. A loud and intrusive sound. She had no intention of answering the phone at all. The ringing simply served as a reminder to have it turned off. She made a mental note to contact the phone company first thing in the morning. *Telemarketers be damned,* she thought.

However, something very unexpected happened. Autumn, her sixteen-year-old daughter, walked into the living room with the cordless phone in tow. Tiffany could tell from the somber expression that this call had meaning. Her big blue eyes widened, and her heart raced. Her initial involuntary thought was that her ex-husband had finally died. A fate that she didn't mind, but then there was Autumn and that would be another heartache. She sat up from the couch and took the receiver.

"Hello" was all Autumn heard her mother say. Tiffany listened intensely as the hairs on her arms and neck rose. Autumn kept hoping for her mother to utter something or make some sort of display that would indicate what she was learning on the other end of the call. Autumn tucked her hair behind her ears with anticipation. Her mother's facial expressions indicated this call was heavy and possibly tragic. Finally, after a few minutes, Tiffany said thank you and hung up. Autumn stopped playing with her hair, clenched her hands, swallowing hard as she prepared for the reveal.

Tiffany cleared her throat and then spoke.

"Your father came out of his coma today." She pressed her hands into her thighs, her eyes fixed on the floor. Tiffany was ordinarily very apathetic concerning Jackson. She no longer hated her ex-husband, but this news flooded her with emotion. Truth be told, Tiffany thought Jackson had met his demise. Maybe she had hoped he would die and be out of their lives forever. Autumn began to weep. Her father was said to be a vegetable, most likely unresponsive and unable to communicate for the rest of his life. She had already grieved him as dead. She wanted to ask her mother a million questions, but all she could think about was the reality that her father was awake.

"Apparently, he has amnesia and doesn't know anything about the accident or his life. He doesn't even know his name," Tiffany offered. Even she could not imagine what Jackson must look like in that hospital bed. Envisioning Jackson helpless, she assumed he could not speak or move freely. Her husband had become a very hard and distant man over the years of their marriage. Yet, Tiffany always saw him as bold, confident and strong. Now she envisioned a man with less than toddler capabilities.

"What does that mean? How long will he not remember anything?"

"There is no way to know," Tiffany stoically answered.

"But he is, ok?" Autumn asked, her voice trembling. Tiffany nodded yes.

"Then we have to go get him," Autumn countered instantly, knowing her mother would reject the idea. Tiffany fell silent as the thought of seeing her ex-husband made her sick to her stomach. Autumn was determined, but she was fully aware of her father's darkness and the pain her mother had endured. She also knew that she would not settle or accept no for an answer. Tiffany looked away, searching for her own defense. She was no longer married to or responsible for Jackson. She owed that man nothing, but her daughter deserved everything. The silence was deafening to both.

"Do you remember the summer I spent with dad several years ago?" the young brown innocent eyes asked. Again, Tiffany nodded yes.

"I hated it with him. I hated being there."

Tiffany just listened and continued to nod.

"But when I met your father in Maryland to pick you up, you cried for over an hour after he left. I thought I would never console you." Tiffany spoke softly.

"I cried because he was still my dad." Autumn let that resonate. She was proving very wise for her years.

"Mom, if we don't go get him, who will?" Her curious and uncertain eyes fixed on her mother.

Tiffany was determined to protect her beautiful offspring and she felt stuck. Tiffany never expected this outcome. All she knew and was warned about was that Jackson would likely not survive. A hardness set in as a way of her own self-preservation. She thought to herself, *only Jackson would refuse to die.*

Cue the Mary Gauthier song, "Mercy Now."

"One condition, and it is non-negotiable."

Autumn's eyebrows raised.

"I go alone. I want to go alone. I think that is the smart thing to do."

Autumn wasn't about to tempt fate. She got up and hugged her mother.

"Just give me a little time to think about this before I commit," Tiffany said as her mind wandered off. She had committed in her heart but wasn't ready to tell her mind.

Autumn left the room. Tiffany was shackled to her doubt. "My life is a dumpster fire," she whispered to no one.

CHAPTER 3

News of the patient in room 777 spread like a prairie brushfire throughout the hospital. An individual waking up from a coma is expected to have struggles and injuries that vary from person to person. Jackson should have muscle atrophy. Jackson should have balance issues, with a high risk of falling, if he was even able to walk at all. He should have no ability to coordinate movements. He should have difficulty speaking, vision problems and trouble swallowing. He should have been in post-traumatic amnesia. His brain shouldn't have been working well and the confusion should have been more profound. Coma patients must relearn their most basic functions, such as brushing their teeth. However, Jackson woke up fully functional and not at all distressed. He could sit up, speak, stand, and most bewildering, walk. This confounded the medical professionals and specialists. What had occurred defied logic, science, and experience. Rumors of a ruse began to stir in the smaller circles of the elite.

Dr. David Selle entered the room. Jackson was sitting up, and Rosemary was visiting with him. Her shift had ended hours ago, but these two were forming a bond. Dr. Selle seemed frail for such a young person, a tall man with a boyish face. The doctor smiled and raised his eyebrows to suggest he was speechless. His huge smile was uncomfortable and somewhat awkward. Selle didn't really have faith in miracles, and in the moment he couldn't explain or understand anything. An intelligent man, he was often charming, enthusiastic, and tireless of his profession. He was determined that this serendipitous moment would not capsize his objectivity.

"Hello, David Selle," Jackson said with a refined, simple, yet amplified tone. He spoke with authority and ease. Selle began shifting his weight from one foot to the other as he often did in unsettling moments.

"Fine doctor, I think I have been poked and prodded by just about every medical professional on staff at this hospital. So, let me guess… is it time for an enema?" Selle's mouth fell open slightly; his patient even had a sense of humor. The doctor just stood in disbelief. His arms were helplessly flailing, his head bobbing. Rosemary and Jackson found the doctor amusing as if he were a child trying to understand. Selle was clearly uncomfortable around Jackson. He felt that Jackson may be more than a miracle, possibly a celestial being. It was normal and necessary for the young doctor to have questions, but where should he begin. David Selle surveyed the room and walked over to a picture on the wall. He leveled it ever so slightly, then began with the only flower arrangement in the room. Jackson sat up straight and observed the doctor. Selle changed the water and then proceeded to emphasize balance, proportion, scale, and harmony. He worked in a circle pulling the larger flowers into the center.

"May I ask what you are doing?" Jackson asked, but it was a rhetorical question. Jackson fully understood the doctor's motivation.

"This is a place of healing," Selle responded.

"And everything matters," Jackson interjected. "What a beautiful culture you all have here."

"You don't gradually come out of a coma after seven weeks and not have so much as a bedsore. People are calling you a marvel; a mystery and all the hospital is a buzz. In a matter of a few hours, you have lit up this hospital like a roman candle."

"Amen to that!" Rosemary spoke with conviction as if she was on a front-row church pew.

"Maybe we are all just seeing things through a different lens," Jackson offered. "Still, so many will doubt because I make no sense. Trust me doctor, I can't explain this any better than you. I can't even tell you who I am, what I am, or where I am from. I can only account for the present which is only a brief part of today."

"What little we know of you is your name, Jackson Martin Riggs. You are from North Carolina. You work for a man named Barry Jenkins. Does that name ring a bell?"

Jackson nodded no.

"Any idea why you would be in Orlando?"

Jackson continued to nod no.

"I don't even know what flavor ice cream I like."

"Mint Chocolate chip, but never the green kind." Rosemary spoke out of turn and Jackson smiled at her.

Selle walked back over and read the monitors. All vital signs remained good, and he listened to Jackson's heart. Doctor Selle grimaced. He gave the equipment a minor inspection and everything seemed to be working fine.

"I am at a loss for words here. There has to be some solid medical evidence or explanation, but you really are the Rubik's Cube of patients."

"Then start with what you do know," Jackson said.

Selle's eyes widened, "I know nothing!"

"What is your favorite flavor?"

Selle looked like a deer frozen in headlights.

"Ice cream, of course."

"Anything with toffee." Selle smiles more sincerely.

People from all over the hospital were peeking in on the spectacle known as Jackson. Selle took note of the onlookers and Jackson seemed unaware or unfazed by the passersby people.

Selle continued, "Can I get you anything?"

"I am hungry. Ice cream maybe. Something with toffee."

Selle handed him a hospital menu. "In the meantime, look this over. Whatever you want. I will make sure you get it right away."

Jackson took the menu and laughed, "As I said, I don't even know what I like."

Jackson studied the menu and then handed it to Rosemary. Without another word she knew she was now his confidante and server. Jackson returned his gaze to Selle, and his expression turned serious. He felt and understood Salle's turmoil. Jackson took Selle and held his shoulders, looking intently into the doctor's eyes.

"Sometimes life is unexplainable. Our ways are not the ways of God. Sometimes there are explanations and at other times not. Sometimes plans work and at other times they don't."

"What do we do in the meantime?"

Jackson smiled. "Live in grace and walk in love. We start with what we know." The two men locked eyes.

"And we extend those principles and practices to people like Dr. Cooper," Jackson interjected. "Not all my buzz is positive." Was Jackson making a statement or asking a

19

question? Selle didn't know. This was surprising to the young doctor.

"I am inquiring about Dr. Alex Cooper. I am not familiar with medical jargon. Obviously, I am not familiar with much, but he is your superior, am I right?"

Dr. Selle simply and uncomfortably gestured his confirmation.

"He actually thinks I am pulling some kind of ruse," Jackson laughed. *How does he know this?* Selle thought. David Selle had had some heated discussions earlier with Alex Cooper. The two doctors were clearly at opposite ends of the spectrum concerning the recovery of Jackson Riggs. Alex Cooper only submitted to logic and science. Selle cited stories of patients' unexplainable recoveries from traumatic strokes and other conditions. He reminded his elder doctor about a man named Burt Gladstone, known in the medical community and journals as the Lazarus patient. Selle spoke like an attorney citing cases and previous laws to a judge. He felt like Atticus Finch from *To Kill a Mockingbird*. Yet, he realized to Dr. Cooper he was probably a lot more like Vinny from the motion picture *My Cousin Vinny*. Alex's heart remained hard and closed to any such explanations. Selle reminded his skeptical superior about the motion picture *Awakenings* starring Robert DeNiro and Robin Williams, but that was to no avail either.

Cooper had organized a panel with a psychiatrist to meet with the miracle patient the following morning. Selle had been tasked with informing Jackson that his presence was being requested at a formal inquiry, an invitation that Selle was uncomfortable extending. Rosemary showed her perplexity. She was never one to be a complicated read. Jackson was staring into and not at his doctor. It was an uneasy silence for the guilt-ridden Selle. Finally, Jackson pulled the bedsheet to his side, rose to his feet, and walked over to Selle. Jackson might as well have been walking on water. His legs should not be able to support his own weight, much less walk. The ever-professional doctor was not prepared for the embrace Jackson gave him. A hug that lasted longer than any had ever for the doctor.

"You are a good man, an amazing doctor, a caring husband, and a wonderful father. Don't allow that incessant guilt to survive inside you. It has been trying to beat you half to death your whole life. That guilt is a lie. As for Cooper, let's not be too quick to see him as an enemy. I don't know what has happened to me, but I can see it in every face that this is extraordinary."

Rosemary watched with wet eyes as Jackson returned to his bed. She had been trained by every hallmark movie ever made to be emotional.

The following day Jackson was dressed in a suit and tie about four sizes too big. She would explain that it had belonged to Rosemary's husband, who had since gone to glory. Though he looked more like a silly hobo in the suit that tried to swallow him, Jackson wore it confidently. He walked into the board room. Doctors David Selle, Steven English, and Alex Cooper, all neurologists, were seated waiting for the Miracle Man to enter.

Along with them was psychologist Dr. Acey Amora. Barely into her thirties, she was proving to be very gifted in her field. She was considered an expert at body language and lie detection reading most people like a cheap drug store novel. Amora believed faces had valuable information and clues into a person's intent and even truths. She maintained that over 4000 facial expressions were made up of just three muscles and had studied all the combinations for well over ten years. Cooper was banking on her to prove Jackson Riggs was a fraud. Next to her was the hospital's Chief Medical Doctor, Dr. Eric Brooks, a stoic man whose faith was in medicine. This hospital was his sanctuary. Cooper had convinced him that Jackson's presumed deception could damage the institution's reputation. Brooks' allegiance was always and would remain to the hospital. Neither man would ever be celebrated for his bedside manner.

Jackson entered unassumingly. His hair was matted down, still wet from his shower. He had no idea how he wore his hair. Rosemary didn't walk behind or lead Jackson but remained right next to him. Dr. Cooper was loud and agitated when he tried to tell Rosemary that she wasn't welcome. This aggravated Jackson greatly and he winced, making his aggravation well understood.
"She is here with me at my invitation... as my guest, confidante, moral support if you will. So, she will be staying". He paused and surveyed the room. "And with that cleared up, we are free to move on and discuss my . . . integrity." When Jackson spoke, it was with an unsettling authority. Again, he didn't look at the doctors; he looked into them. He could understand things and know things that felt intrusive even to himself. Then just as quickly he returned to resiliency and optimism.
Doctor Cooper was the first to speak.
"Allow me to introduce you to everyone here," he said as he turned to the psychiatrist to his left. "This is..." Cooper tried to finish, but Jackson cut him off.
"I know who she is, Alex, and I know why she is here. Doctor Amora's maiden name is Clemena, am I right?"

23

Jackson had started a habit of putting his statements in the form of a question. Cooper found it insulting how Jackson addressed him, which wasn't unnoticed by the others in the conference room.

"The truth is, Alex, Dr. Amora has already concluded I am not lying. I am not some elaborate ruse. Though she will admit I am somewhat unexplainable right now. For that matter, who wouldn't agree with her." Jackson turned his gaze to Dr. Amora.

"Dr. Amora, you are bored to death working at this hospital and are longing to get into something like criminal psychology. This is odd considering your love of marine biology, but I suppose we all have multiple interests. I want to assure you…you will excel in that field just as you have here for the past four years. You are attractive, funny, and smart. Your smile serves this hospital well. It needs doctors like you and Dr. Selle. But you will be leaving, and that you must do for yourself. You two, being younger, are not suffering from the same 'paralysis from analysis' that your superiors are victims of. You both still have questions as opposed to accusations. I don't have answers, and I thank you for believing me. It does kind of suck to be your own enigma. However, before you leave, I need a favor."

The room was a gasp, but Jackson took no interest or concern in their formalities. Instead, he pointed to Dr. Steven English.

"You are a good man but a broken man. Life has clearly side-swiped you leaving you alone and very lonely. You have a bit of a drinking problem, and you are forming other bad habits as well. On the other hand, you have been very successful with patients and people important to you. So please Dr. English, refocus on yourself." He turned back to Acey. "You both love the same type of motion pictures. Steven needs a friend like you".

Jackson turned his attention back to Dr. Alex Cooper. "Alex, be faithful in all things and relationships." Jackson looked directly into Cooper's eyes until the doctor broke away to look around the room. Jackson felt no need to explain his statement. "Dr. Brooks, you can relax. I am not here to share secrets, but I will be more than displeased if Dr. English lacks your full support." All the men in the room were uncomfortable, but the two women felt at ease with Jackson. It was obvious that Jackson was about correction but never condemnation.

Dr. Alex Cooper abruptly stood up.

"Take your seat, Dr. Cooper," Dr. Brooks instructed and a brewing incident came to a halt.

"Doctor Brooks, I mean this establishment no harm. I mean no one in this room any harm, but I want your assurance that Steven will be helped and protected."

"You must understand, Mr. Riggs, you have a reputation. But, of course, what we may have heard is all hearsay, I mind you. Still, at times, the stories can be both alarming as well as provocative." Dr. Brooks spoke calmly.

Jackson stood still. He was a man of no reputation. How could he proceed? What could he offer this hospital staff that would be concrete?

"You are a man. In fact, everyone in this room is an individual with extraordinary instincts and insights. I have things to do that are pressing and do not involve any of you. So again, I appreciate your help in these matters."

Jackson announced that the inquisition was over. He escorted Rosemary out of the room. The dumbfounded doctors looked at one another in disbelief. When Dr. Cooper tried to question Dr. Brooks about why he allowed Jackson complete control of the room, he was dismissed once more.

Jackson's hand touched the door handle as Brooks called out with one last question. "What is so important, Mr. Riggs, that you must get to?"

Jackson smiled, "I don't know," and he began to exit.

"Some secrets are better left unsaid," is all Brooks offered.

"Before you go, Mr. Riggs, I want you to know we contacted your wife about your recovery," Cooper offered.
Jackson froze and turned back to face the men.
"I am married?"
"Well, your ex-wife."
Jackson didn't exactly know what to do with this information. He felt like a child lost in the dark.
Up until this moment, he had been undeservingly kind, and he hemorrhaged control even when there was tension in the conference room. All the others knew that Jackson was full of goodness in their hearts and minds. It was as if he were completely deliberate in his presentation, and now, he was the one that captivated his audience in a new way.
"And children?"
"I understand you have a daughter named Autumn." Even the infuriated Cooper had softened seeing Jackson so childlike.

    Cue: The John Mayer song, "Daughters."
"Autumn. Wow." Jackson spoke delicately and walked out of the room.

CHAPTER 4

Tiffany got up the next morning and went for a run. She had a lot of anxiety to burn off. Although she wanted nothing to do with her ex-husband, it was more important that she protect her daughter's heart. A living Jackson Riggs opened the aqueduct of nightmares that no eyes should see. Her ex-husband always managed to bring doom to every situation. He was in a world of chaos and Autumn was naïve to expect anything different. Tiffany was not the type to betray her own logic. He was not just painful to their daughter, but Tiffany knew he was futile. Her thoughts were racing ahead of her feet as she ran faster than usual. "What was Jackson Riggs doing in Orlando, Florida anyway?" she wondered. Having no doubt that the answer would be disturbing and disgusting to her, she found herself tempted to resent her daughter, but how could she? The realization was a cruel one. Tiffany had to go to Florida. Any other way would never do for Autumn. Tiffany was the one who had made the choice to marry the man. Autumn was never given the privilege of choosing. A concoction of guilt and self-hatred began to stir within her soul.

Walking back into her home, Tiffany met Autumn in the kitchen. There was a lingering awkward silence. They both knew the teenager was awaiting an answer. Tiffany had made up her mind but was reluctant. She felt trapped and obligated. Every cell in her body was screaming no.

Autumn continued to sit silently and eat her toaster strudel. Her mother started making a smoothie. It was a violent undertaking. Tiffany tossed the ingredients into the blender with force while flinging shut the cabinets and refrigerator door. When the smoothie was finished, she drank straight from the pitcher, slammed it onto the counter, and cursed under her breath about forgetting her protein powder. Silently she wished this smoothie had a healthy serving of vodka. The feelings running circles in her brain called for mixed drinks. She knew that children had an optimistic view by nature.

Cue: The Eric Church song, "Holdin' My Own".

Stoically, she pulled herself together. It felt like slow motion when she turned to face her daughter.
"I will go," is all she said.

CHAPTER 5

A few days had passed, and Jackson's continued stay in the hospital was not making any sense. Dr. Selle had asked the patient to stay for observation. Jackson agreed because he still had no idea where he would go. Rosemary was turning into his roommate, but even she had to return to her life at some point. Still, the patient of room 777 had no worry or foreseeable thought about any other time but now. He did not live in fear of tomorrow or the future.

The two had taken to playing Gin Rummy regularly, and today, Rosemary was beating him. He had asked her to introduce him to music, so she gave him an iPhone with Spotify. He was introduced to everything from Beethoven to The Beatles, from gospel to country. She often felt amazed that a man with such resolve could also be as inquisitive as a three-year-old. Despite the dingy, yellow hospital walls, the room was filled with joy. Other patients would routinely stop in and visit with the one many called "the miracle man."

They came to hear his story firsthand. Some visitors were hoping for comforting words to ease the pain of their own sorrow and challenges. The visits were not always easy. Many elderlies were losing loved spouses after years of marital bliss. A lot of people were saying goodbye on account of death being imminent. Jackson's defining moment occurred when speaking to an older gentleman. His name was Bernie, and he had been married to his beloved Melody for forty-seven years. Bernie slouched over and shuffled his feet. His white head of hair was full and styled much like Grandpa Munster from the old television series. His clothes were old and had been out of fashion for years, but they were in mint condition. He walked over and the two locked eyes. For the very first time, Rosemary excused herself from the room. Bernie's eyes filled with tears. Jackson took both of the older man's hands. "She wants to go tonight. She wants you to say goodbye. She is tired Bernie." Bernie's lip quivered. "I know it is hard but try to see her as part of your future, not your past. You will see her again on the other side." Bernie smiled softly.

    Another visitor was no surprise. A woman came and silently stood in the doorframe. Her long flowing blonde hair, her brown eyes, and her sun-kissed skin were the most angelic sight Jackson had ever seen. Slowly he stood to his feet. Rosemary marveled at the adoration in his eyes. She was wearing white jeans and a navy top. Her face was expressionless as the two just stood and studied each other. Tiffany was confident Jackson knew her immediately; however, years of pain kept her blind to his awe of her. Love's hurts have a way of keeping score.

"Hello," he said softly. Rosemary was still captivated at the sight of Jackson's wonder. Tiffany had not heard a soft tone from the man in years. Silently, she reminded herself of all her reasons to hate him. The roster was long, and the memories flooded her soul.

"May I ask who you are?" he questioned softly.

Rosemary stood to her feet and while walking towards Jackson asked, "You don't know who she is?" It was the first time since his awakening that he needed any introduction. Jackson just knew people's names. Just like he knew Rosemary's name the moment his eyes opened. He nodded no without breaking his gaze away from Tiffany. Then, turning to their visitor, Rosemary explained, "He tends to know stuff like this."

Jackson walked closer to Tiffany and took her hand. He held it and closed his eyes. Usually, Jackson could see things about people, but she was a blank page. He knew nothing, and he found himself in unfamiliar territory since he woke from the coma. Eventually, Tiffany snatched her hand out of his.

"You know me? You were part of my life before, weren't you?" he asked. Suddenly his lucid sight turned obscure.

"I am your ex-wife, the mother of your only child. At least I suspect your only child, who knows with you," Tiffany said. She was uncomfortable with the way Jackson looked at her. His eyes were kind, and that was not who he had been. She felt like she was in a cruel version of *The Twilight Zone*. Tiffany stepped back. The woman had become a girl in the way she looked away. Her sensitivity had built fences and Jackson did not honor the boundaries. "May we go for a walk?" he asked sheepishly.

A walk, she shouted with her inner voice. They had not been on a walk in years before their divorce. She reasoned her ex-husband must be desperate for a chaperone. Yet she had to admit that his resilience and audacity were charming. She thought of him as a hobo and a child with aristocratic tendencies. Was she prepared for a conversation with this new man's river of thought? She found herself in a world within a world of tranquility. She felt an unfamiliar peace as he led her out the door.

    Once they went out of the front door of the hospital, Jackson froze and took deep breaths. The smell of fresh Florida air seemed new yet familiar. It was the first time he had been outside since he arrived at Orlando Health. Tiffany was both amused and embarrassed watching Jackson. It was early April, so the heat had yet to conquer the air. The landscaping was immaculate, and greenery was everywhere. He walked over to a tall man in his early sixties smoking a cigarette by a water fountain. Tiffany immediately felt stranded, a feeling she knew very well coming from Jackson. Leaving her behind had always come easy to him.

"Excuse me, but is there a park nearby? A place where we can see some more of this beauty?" He waved his hand at the landscape. Tiffany watched her stranger of an ex-husband, who was an insatiable presence. The man's name was Hal and he had never seen anyone like Jackson. Tiffany was fascinated and walked closer to be sure she was hearing him correctly. The douchebag of a man she knew was never kind to strangers and always asked questions as if stating a command.

"There is, about two or three miles north of here off Orange Avenue, beside a big lake called Lake Eola."

"Thank you, Hal," Jackson said as he motioned for Tiffany to start walking with him. She was riveted by this version of Jackson. How did he know this man, Hal? She followed him. As they were about to cross Orange Avenue, Hal's big Mercury stopped next to them. The window lowered, and the kind gentleman offered to drive them to the park.

As Hal pulled into a small parking lot on the east side of the park, he explained that some quaint restaurants were a few blocks over. Hal was proving to be an excellent tour director. Jackson thanked the kind stranger once again.

"I assume you two are returning to the hospital after this?" Hal asked.

Jackson looked to Tiffany as she nodded yes.

"Then I will just wait here for you lovebirds," Hal offered.

"Oh no, no, we are not lovebirds, sir," Tiffany interjected uncomfortably.

"I am afraid I am her ex-husband as tragic as that is to admit. Even worse, I don't think she likes me very much. It's kind of a funny story... you see I have amnesia," but Jackson couldn't continue.

Hal smiled. "I suspected you were the Miracle Man. Stories have been all over town about you. I even read something in The Orlando Sentinel. You are famous. So, you two take that walk, and I will be right here. No hurries, no worries."

As they exited the car Hal spoke up one more time, "May I ask how you knew my name?"

"He sees everything in front of him but nothing behind him," Tiffany said with a grin. Then she looked away knowing in her heart that the promise of this new man would bring much disappointment when the real man returned.

Walking in the park north of the hospital, the two strangers were more than a little awkward. Jackson was momentarily at a loss for words.

"May I ask why we divorced?" Jackson inquired.

Tiffany remained silent, and she pondered the question. Should she be honest? There were things she had always wanted to say to Jackson. Feelings about her hurt and broken dreams and the many tears she cried, but he was too narcissistic to even bother listening. Should she tell him of his affairs? Should she tell him that although he provided financially for Autumn, he was still a deadbeat dad? Should she tell him he had become a man that could watch a person bleed to death and never feel compassion or empathy? Should she tell him the stories she had heard of his crooked business dealings? His greatest skill was intimidating and strong-arming the most powerful of people. However, now she was walking with a man that had become the great unknown. Dr. Selle had shared some stories about Jackson. While he was asleep in a coma, no one visited him, sent cards or flowers, and he was a John Doe for the first several days. Almost a week later, Jackson's room was filled with cards, letters, balloons, and flowers from people he had never met. The news of the Miracle Man had a strong word of mouth and social media had taken to his story very kindly. Still, this was not the man she knew. She had a heap of explanations and discoveries for Jackson. *What would these past truths do to serve him or her*, she wondered.

Furthermore, Doctor Selle could not predict when or even if Jackson would get his memory back. She thought about the motion picture *Awakenings*, starring Robin Williams and Robert DeNiro. In that film, the character came out of a catatonic state but eventually returned to his debilitating condition. Now the question loomed...how long before Jackson returned to his old self? When would his words become daggers, belittling others while breaking their daughter's heart again? What would be the point of sharing his past? In his current condition, Jackson was a stranger to both. Shattered dreams and a broken heart turned to stone were all she had to offer, but now everything seemed to be shifting in the sand. It was another time, and they were out of place. She remained silent and conflicted. Her inner monologue and narrative prose were congested. Worst yet, when the fury and fire of the old Jackson ever returned, how would he react to her answers. Silence was simply best. She stopped and looked at the huge fountain in the middle of a man-made lake. They were standing in front of the smaller amphitheater. She returned her gaze to Jackson and thought of how absolutely unique he had become.

Jackson had waited for her reply but sensed accurately that anything she had to offer would mostly only trigger her bad memories.

"I must say your eyebrows are perfect...wonderfully placed above your beautiful brown eyes." He spoke so gently that she wasn't sure if he wanted to be her father or her lover. She looked away, her eyes watering, but she would not dare cry in front of him. She was adrift in this new territory.

"I am sorry if I upset you." There was an air of mischief about him. The possibilities and her natural beauty humbled him. She looked away again, this time at the green water of sage and sycamore the lake provided. She listened to the wind whistle around and thought, *my eyebrows. My eyebrows! How could he know that I labor over eyebrows every night?* The truth was that Jackson didn't know, but he knew she was the most beautiful sight he had ever seen. Jackson was sure that he must have felt she was the most beautiful woman alive even before his accident. Yet, he could see nothing of their past, or even inside her. Why was she so blank to him? As they walked and passed people, he could see right into these total strangers, but the only real link to his past was locked like a steel door. As with all steel doors, he knew what was on the other side was very valuable to him.

There were homeless people, owners walking pets and couples picnicking all around. They felt as if they were the only two anywhere in sight. Feelings of happiness kept coming in waves, but Tiffany always reminded herself that reality was sinister. She tried to stay in the moment, but the neurosis of past failures remained involved.

"May I ask why you came here?" His question was loaded with expectation.

Tiffany told him about their daughter. He asked to see her picture and thought she was mesmerizingly beautiful. She resembled him much more than Tiffany.

"She clearly has your eyebrows."

Yet another well-placed and perfect compliment, she thought. She might even miss this version of Jackson when the old one returned. Her mind knew better than to think this was a moment of innocence.

She continued to explain that it was Autumn who had insisted she come. Nothing in Tiffany's life was arbitrary. Her nature is very analytical. Everything is well thought out in her life. Her decision to visit Jackson was a slow process and included careful consideration. Even among the twinges of old memories she knew their daughter wanted her father to find his way home. Tiffany was there to get him back to Raleigh, North Carolina. This was to be a rare gesture, but meaningful for Autumn. She knew he wouldn't remember, but she still asked why he had come to Orlando in the first place.

Nevertheless, Jackson had no idea. A quick exploration of his memories left him with nothing. He longed for nostalgia, but amnesia doesn't offer that. He did not even know where the accident took place. The focus had been consumed on his recovery and not the accident. Yet now Tiffany was here, and it was time to let her questions begin. She didn't yet realize that the empty past meant nothing to Jackson. His attention and devotion to her were strange and she liked it. She looked at him knowing that inevitable changes were ahead. She could not understand her desire for him. Eventually the threshold of a new love story would disappear. Soon they would be different people once more, or were they already?

It was time to find clarity in how to bring this woman retribution. All he knew was that he was filled with a love and passion for this Tiffany. Her long blonde hair was whipped around by the wind. Even the subtlety of how she tucked her hair behind her ears was attractive. He wanted to love her well. Was it that the old self had fallen out of love or changed, but the vow never died? He had no idea why she was a stranger, a mystery and even a muse, but Tiffany held him captive. His heart was in chaos that he had failed her. What was next? He had no idea. Yet, he was certain that this was his purpose even if she never included him in her life as a husband, lover, or friend.

"Tell me this," Jackson's tone shifted. "Have we ever been to a concert?"

Tiffany laughed. She looked at Jackson to answer and laughed again. An abrupt shift in conversation, also so unlike his old self. Jackson's curiosity rose, as did his eyebrows.

"Why would you ask that?"

"Rosemary has been using Spotify to help reintroduce me to music. I like music."

"We saw a few," she paused and laughed again. She pulled herself together. "We saw two shows where you absolutely embarrassed me. They were Garth Brooks and Bruce Springsteen. You sang every word of their songs and jammed out all night long."

"Was I drunk?"

She laughed again in her response. "No, that was what made it so sad."

Jackson had found his link and continued to ask her questions that he knew would lead to funny answers. His plan was working, and the intensity of their conversation lightened.

"There is something else your doctor and I discussed today," she said. Jackson perked up in surprise. She explained that she was there to take him home and they were leaving this evening. She would escort him to his apartment. There was no reason for him to stay at the hospital any longer. Jackson knew being released was near, but he was still surprised it was upon him. He tried again to panic, but the peace cut into his every doubt. He smiled. "Then there are some things we need to do before I can go," he said.

CHAPTER 6

Rosemary walked into his hospital room realizing her favorite patient's stay was over. The two embraced. Jackson then walked over and filled both women's hands with flowers, balloons, or whatever they could carry.

"Find the patients that don't have any sign of family and make sure you leave these things with them. And don't rush, visit."

Tiffany was again uncomfortable. "What am I supposed to say to these people?" she asked.

Jackson smiled. He knew the gesture required nothing to be said. It was only important that they share and show love.

"Well, that is the simplest part. You don't have to say anything. Rosemary will go with you. We do this all the time, but we just can't seem to empty this room out."

Jackson was again speaking with authority, but he was not a bully like his old self. In fact, his tone was encouraging in some odd way. This new version of him was hardly mundane.

Rosemary grinned as she took Tiffany's hand. She was never one to refuse a friendship.

Tiffany looked around at the room filled with gifts. She could not imagine giving all these things away, not to mention visiting with complete strangers.

Jackson could not read or see into Tiffany like the others, but the expression on her face made her resistance clear. He looked deep into her eyes again, admiring her eyebrows.

"The purpose of these things is to bring comfort. I don't need them anymore. I need to pass them on."

"Why?"

"The mind can't subtract things. Aside from Dementia, Alzheimer's or in my case, amnesia, the mind only adds. To heal we must replace old hurts with new experiences. These simple gestures for so called strangers create replacement memories. You see our destinies are not meaningless coincidences. These people are part of our journey, and we are a part of theirs."

She shrugged. How could she argue? There was a time she wished he was this kind, but she never thought she would have to step out of her comfort zone.

"Kind of like the movie, *Pay It Forward*?"

"I am sure you will share that with me one day."

Rosemary was more than proud to be chosen to escort Tiffany. She felt like the most cherished woman in the world for Jackson to have so much faith in her.

Tiffany's walls came crumbling down when she saw the elderly patients who had outlived their loved ones. What Tiffany thought was inappropriate and intrusive just proved to be joyful and fulfilling. Rosemary watched Tiffany enjoy her involvement. She fully felt the impact of boosting morale, providing comfort, and offering indescribable relief that patients felt in an otherwise cold and sterile environment. She was surprised at the support the hospital staff gave Jackson. This umbrella of influence was huge, and she grew to cherish her involvement. Tiffany left a patient's room after listening to an elderly man talk of his love for his wife who had passed years ago. He shared that no other woman could replace her. The man had chosen to stay lonely because, to him, that was what it meant to be faithful. Tiffany was almost running back to room 777 when Rosemary said, "No, come with me." Tiffany once again was caught off guard. There was still so much more joy to share...why interrupt the cycle? Today was proving to be filled with beautiful discoveries. So, she followed Rosemary, who led her to a room where they found Jackson sitting on the edge of a woman's bed.

From outside the doorway, the two women watched as Jackson gently held her hand. The woman was fragile and had even outlived her own children. Tiffany could not hear their words, just occasional laughter. She watched Jackson lift her frail hand and kiss it before he wrapped his arms around her, giving her a warm embrace. He was fully engaged, and Tiffany was caught between disbelief and admiration. Her most hated human being was sharing a love that people would never forget. Once Rosemary realized that Tiffany was seeing a unique man, she took her by the arm and the two left. Once again, Jackson was clueless that Tiffany was just outside, but if only he could see her clever and inquisitive glances. Rosemary, clutching Tiffany's arm much like a grandmother, shared a story with her. Jackson had said to Rosemary just the other day, "It is easy to fall in love with people's smiles, but what they are really looking for is someone to love their scars."

Cue the Rascal Flatts song, "My Wish."

The day ended with hugs, tears, and small promises. The kind of promises that gave way to fate.

CHAPTER 7

The hospital was now part of his past. He was at the airport and a funny sight he proved to be. For Jackson seeing things for the first time again made him very childlike. Tiffany had to teach him how to get on an escalator. Moving stairs and walkways fascinated Jackson. For a man so driven in profession, ambition, and even recreation he was now eerily free, she noticed.

They arrived at their terminal. Jackson spoke less now, but not because he was awkward. He was just soaking in his surroundings. Every aspect of the airport interested him. He noticed people and always seemed to be looking much deeper than their outward appearance. His fascination amused Tiffany. He was so intrigued by everything. She again forgot the apathy she had felt toward him for years.

Suddenly Jackson became engrossed, almost like a predator searching out prey. His expressions of wonder had changed, but she could not make sense of them. Jackson rose to his feet and took her hand. With no explanation, Jackson led Tiffany over to a man. His clothing, a traditional vestment, made it clear he was a Catholic priest. Jackson sat next to the man disregarding the many empty available seats. Tiffany kept clutching

Jackson's hand, indicating that she was uncomfortable. Jackson ignored her. He was fixated, and for a moment, he reminded her of his cruel and careless self.

"Are you ever going to tell him?" Jackson asked the priest. Jackson was in the priest's space now and he continued, "acceptance, although hardly glamorous, is the most important part of love."

"I am sorry, son. I don't understand." The priest was accustomed to strangers approaching him about their problems, questions, and fears.

"Why haven't you of all people told God you are mad at him? It isn't as if he doesn't know?"

"Son, God is never wrong."

"No, he is not, but that does not mean a person will not hold feelings of resentment toward God for a decision they do not understand; His ways are not our ways. You can believe in the sovereignty of God and still be angry with him. For the healing to begin, you must tell him you are angry and that you do not understand."

The situation became difficult for the priest and Tiffany, but Jackson never so much as blinked an eye.

"He knows. Just talk to him, ok?"

The priest was easily twenty-five years older than Jackson. Yet, his eyes filled with the emotion of a child and all of his suspicions fell away. He relaxed. A peace came over him even though he felt he was being read like a cheap drug store novel.

"You know that thing you guys do... confession? You have the right idea. Confessing your sins is good, but it's to be done so that the confessor can hear they are forgiven and loved. Tell God you need Him to forgive you. It is way past time".

Jackson stood and waited on the priest to rise. Jackson did not ask or give any indication that he was going to hug this stranger, but he did. He held on loosely, but the hug lingered.

"You truly believe we are created in God's image?" Jackson asked.

The priest nodded yes.

"Then talk to him and understand that He knows all the feelings you struggle with." Jackson spoke in the most calming way. Nothing else needed to be said. The two men who were strangers connected on a level of emotional depth that left Tiffany in awe.

Walking away Jackson stopped and returned to the older man.

"The biggest injustice to prayer is that we have made it a formula as opposed to a conversation. Stop trying to impress God. Your redemption isn't in your work. You were created for relationship."

On the plane seated next to each other, Tiffany was flooded with questions. The sound of her mind's wheels turning was making her crazy.

"Why was that man mad at God?" she asked.

Jackson paused before he answered.

"It may not be my place to share his private and personal business."

"But you can walk up to him, be vague and possibly even embarrass him publicly?" she countered.

He kept silent.

"Or you don't know? You simply guessed? Isn't everybody mad at a God they interpret as an absentee landlord?"

Unexpectedly, the stewardess walked up to the unconnected couple. "Mr. and Mrs. Riggs, a gentleman has upgraded your seats to first-class if you will accept."

Jackson looked at Tiffany for approval.

"Really?" was all she could utter.

Once settled into first-class, Jackson asked the priest if he could share his story with Tiffany. Even the priest still questioned Jackson's authenticity, but he allowed it. Jackson explained that before Tom had joined the priesthood, he was a father to a son named Eric. Eric had fallen off the side of a mountain on a rock-climbing expedition. Shortly after, Tom's marriage died too, and he later joined the clergy. Tom joined looking for answers;

however, he never found them in a God that allowed the death of his son. In the clergy, Tom was a gift to everyone he met. He made people feel loved and accepted, but he never got the answers he wanted, and his anger lingered. Soon after sharing, Jackson looked at Tiffany and said, "Those are the sweetest eyes I have ever seen." She paused. *Was he being romantic, or just kind of desperate?* He would not break his gaze from her.

"Please tell me, who was I?"

The words came slowly as she thought but eventually offered, "You were everything and yet nothing."

CHAPTER 8

They arrived at the Raleigh-Durham International airport at 11:11pm. Walking to her car he took notice of her Toyota Prius, the most current year of the company's model hybrid. The car was different. He asked and she explained that it was supposed to be eco-friendly. He was fascinated when she explained you could plug the car in to charge it. He wondered how passionate she was about wanting to protect the environment, but he knew she didn't appear to enjoy too many questions. Again he thought, how had he hurt this woman? Had it been all his doing or was it a series of decisions gone wrong? His only certainty was that she had no interest in elaborating.

The door of the car opened. His eyes went straight up the side of the building. Jackson tried counting the floors to his downtown home. He was a little taken aback and surprised to see he lived in such luxury, and he had not even been inside yet.

"Do I own one of these or rent?" he asked.

"I am not sure," she responded flatly. "You never shared any details of your life when I divorced you. For that matter, you didn't tell me too much when we were married," Tiffany continued. Being back on her home turf was changing her demeanor towards him. Similar surroundings reminded her more of the old Jackson and erased the newer version she met earlier that afternoon. She was tired. This was perhaps the longest day of her life. "You didn't ask questions today about Autumn." Her tone was almost bitter. He paused, but she felt he was stalling. She grimaced.

"You didn't want me to yet."

How did he know, she thought. He didn't; it was a strategic guess.

The downtown area was pristine. There were lots of little quaint specialty restaurants and stores. Jackson noticed he lived on Fayetteville Street. He invited Tiffany up, but she respectfully declined, offering him a folded piece of paper. She explained that these were some helpful contacts. His staff, colleagues, assistant, and driver were scribbled down. It did not go unnoticed that Tiffany made no mention of family or friends. She hugged him and he felt distanced from her even before she drove off.

The elevator doors opened, and the eleventh floor greeted him. He had a very humble little bag from his stay in Orlando. Dropping his luggage to the ground, he walked into the living room. It was a wide and spacious area with an amazing panoramic view. There was impressive artwork on the walls, but no family pictures anywhere. There were expensive things all around, but the condo was barren of personal items. There were absolutely no clues to his past or personality. He thought his home looked more like a furniture showroom.

The kitchen was open to the living room, and it lacked nothing. Equipped with every modern appliance, Jackson supposed he might be a chef. Maybe he just cooked as a hobby. However, when he investigated his cabinets, he saw empty shelves except for a few bottles of Fiji water. He opened the refrigerator and again discovered bare shelves, with one lone bottle of Fiji water in the door. Jackson made the safe assumption that he did not entertain guests at his home.

All three of the bedrooms looked very similar. Though the master suite was larger than the others, it was barely distinguished. Artwork, both famous and unknown, dressed the walls. However, the view of the city was not what he was most fond of. He was too high for the city lights to stalk the windows. But again, all things were in their proper place. Nothing gave any indication of his character, his career or even his interests. The condo looked perfectly like a model home, and although pleasing to the eye, no warmth could be felt.

Jackson's next excursion took him to the rooftop, where he discovered a pool and a spectacular fireplace. The view of the city was stunning. He had all of this, yet his formal self was alone and to the new Jackson that was sad. He sat studying the city. Dr. David Selle had mentioned that once back in familiar surroundings his memory might begin to kick in. Selle used the metaphor "much like jumper cables bring a car's battery back to life," but sometimes the battery can't sustain the charge. Well, Jackson was still his mystery. There had been no revelation inside his home...only more questions. He wanted to be frustrated and question his problem, but that peace enveloped him again. The same peace that kept visiting him since he woke up from the coma. His instinct was to question why he could not muster worry, but he just rested again. It was as if Jackson had no needs unmet.

He reached into his pocket and revisited the list of people Tiffany had written for him. He admired her handwriting for a few moments...the big loopy way she jotted her words. She dotted her i's with little hearts. He pulled the paper to his nose and breathed in slowly and deeply. It was there, rather faint, but her captivating fragrance was on the paper. Suddenly it occurred to him she must still be there too. Maybe Tiffany was in the distance, but she was there somewhere. This gave birth to an early morning idea. Person number one on his list was Jim Adams. As a result, the first call Jackson made was to his driver.

Jim Adams arrived at 203 Fayetteville Street precisely 37 minutes later. Jim would usually be dressed appropriately, but Jackson insisted that he not waste any time. The limo pulled up street side and Jim was out of the car immediately to open his boss' door. It was not uncommon for Jackson to need rides at odd times of the day and holidays were no exception. Jim and Jackson stood face to face on the sidewalk. The driver could not help but notice his passenger seemed displeased.

"Jim, what do you drive?"

"Mr. Riggs," Jim began but was immediately interrupted.

"Call me Jackson." He spoke with sweetness, but he was firm.

"A Honda Civic, sir."

"What is my name?"

"Jackson, sir."

The strangers laughed together. The rebuke was polite. Now first names were the new rule, but even Jackson understood old habits die hard.

"Do you know where Tiffany lives?" he paused. "I don't even know her last name," he continued, "Did she return to her maiden name Herzog?"

However, Jim knew exactly who Tiffany was and where she lived. So, the two immediately got in the car and drove into the darkness.

Tiffany and Autumn lived on Poolside Court in North Raleigh. Her neighborhood seemed inviting and very middle class. Walking up to the door he already envied the friendliness of her home. The Cape Cod-style house was on a hill, and he immediately found it engaging. It was in the heart of North Raleigh but still had a small-town feel.

Tiffany was in bed. The house was dark, but she was wide awake. Replaying her ex-husband's every gesture, his smile, and his tone he felt like a ghost that she could not shake from her thoughts. The sound that broke her concentration was faint but a rude interruption of her reflection. Was someone knocking at her door at this hour, she wondered? That was impossible, she reasoned, but the sound was persistent. She got out of bed and put on her robe. She walked to the front window and saw a Limo parked in front of her house. The butterflies in her stomach collided with the annoyance of her reason. It was Jackson and he had no right to be so intrusive. She took a moment and worked up her temper. She had to be firm as she stormed downstairs to tell him off. Every step she took was met with words of scolding as she rehearsed her tongue lashing. She reminded herself that they were no longer in Orlando, and it was time to leave pleasantries behind.

She flung the door open. Jackson saw her disheveled look, make-up free revealing her natural beauty. Even in rage her blue eyes sent a lightning strike to his heart. He did not speak; he gasped. A nervous feeling ran up his spine. The innocence in his eyes and gaze left her speechless. He was stunned and motionless, gazing in awe at her beauty. Finally, she broke the silence when she asked why he was on her front porch at such an outrageous hour. She felt her muscles tighten, fighting against her own weakness.

"I realized in the park this morning; I never asked you your favorite song." Jackson was too tactful to say much. She wanted to be aggravated with him, but that would require a lot of work on her part. Her emotions clouded her instincts. She couldn't even claim the righteous honor of being wronged by this man so many times. The woman became a girl and answered.

"Walking in Memphis."

"Also, I was wondering if I could borrow our wedding album, videos and anything else you might have." He spoke so softly and kind she could not bring herself to say, "screw you." Instead, she tried hanging on to the memory that would keep her hidden behind her bitter ache. Yet, her former anger could not help her rise above this child-like man.

"Why?" she asked eyes squinting. Jackson explained that there was absolutely no evidence of who he was in his condominium; no hints to his person at all. He was hoping she could help.

Tiffany shut the door only to return several minutes later. Jackson had no idea if her closing the door was the answer "no" to his question. He was surprised when she returned with two shoeboxes. Inside one was their wedding video and the other was filled with love letters he had written her during their courtship. He looked down at the boxes as if he was holding a fragile infant. In his hands he held a strong link to the past. He almost trembled at the thought of his past and revelations that he was holding, but that inner peace never gave away. His eyes rose to meet Tiffany's once more.

He could not see into her like he could other people, but she was never certain. Jackson could not keep his eyes off her, having no fear of eye contact. He was not afraid of an awkward silence. In fact, Tiffany suspected he might like the quietness and gentle meaning behind nonverbal communication. He took her hand and squeezed it. It was amazing how she felt his gratitude in the touch. His grip was not weak or too strong. As he walked away, she thought of him as a one-man army that was also a child. Jackson stopped. He turned to her one

more time. He paused and was silent again. Tiffany envied and hated how silence didn't disturb him. He was looking up at her from the bottom of steps.
"You are so beautiful; you make everyone around you beautiful too." She felt like she was the stranger when he said those words. Those epidemic swirls of futile rage she tried to hold onto kept disintegrating.

She closed the door and turned to find her sleepy-eyed daughter. Of course, the question followed, who was at the door and what was her mother doing. "I have no idea," was all Tiffany could offer. There was no way Jackson suddenly knew right from wrong, but he sure knew how to do everything his way.

In the car as they drove away, Jim was silent.
"Play me the song, "Walking in Memphis," please.
Cue the Marc Cohn song, "Walking in Memphis."

CHAPTER 9

Back at his condo on Fayetteville Street, Jackson had spent the last couple hours engrossed in studying his previous life story. Every letter he read made him wonder where and when he had lost Tiffany. Had he also lost himself? He was impressed with the letters and cards he had written. He could not imagine that he left her. He had seen her with his new eyes, and no one shined like she did. It was a sad and absurd situation he felt.

Sitting on the couch he heard someone enter through the front door. An unwelcome intrusion or had Tiffany come to visit him this time? He walked to the foyer. There stood a woman, but she was not his Tiffany. Their eyes met, but this time the silence was very different. He studied the perfectly manicured woman who stood still in a long overcoat. Everything about her was visibly perfect. Her very essence was beautiful. Unexpectedly she dropped her coat to the floor, revealing a matching green bra and panty against her dark skin. She was tall and slender, and her long hair was dark chocolate brown and perfect.

"I suspect I have seen you like this a thousand times," he asked.

She nodded yes and walked to him. He walked towards and past her to pick up her overcoat. She seemed nervous. He draped the coat over her and invited her in. She immediately felt that he was being more attentive than he had ever been before. This was just so unusual and unsettling. It had never been her custom to speak to Jackson before he spoke. He would lead and she would follow in the same fashion and experience of dance partners. Also, like a perfectionist dance partner, Jackson always refused to respond to anything less than ideal. He led her to a seat and then took his place on the couch. He kept trying to see inside her, but maybe the gift was gone? Whenever he needed this gift to serve him it did not work. He explained about his amnesia. However, she had already knew about that. She knew everything about him. He discovered her name to be Tracey Lewan. She glanced at the shoe boxes and the contents spread around, but still very neat. Jackson had questions and it was now her time to share.

      He learned that Tracey had flown to Orlando with him. However, when he inquired about the visit, he realized that his business was always off limits to her. She was never permitted to ask about anything. He guarded his secrets and privacy with viciousness. Yet, she was able to assure him that it was a business trip. On the airplane they had a minor argument when she suggested they take some time to visit Clearwater or even a theme park. She simply wanted time with her lover outside of the bedroom. She wanted to feel value versus the shallowness of the arm candy he had reduced her to. However, the old Jackson saw leisure activities that did not serve his ambitions as a waste of time. He simply had had no interest in her wants or needs. The proposition made Jackson angry so much that once they landed at Orlando International Airport, he immediately purchased her a first-class ticket back home. Tracey had never even left the airport. "I sat alone crying in the terminal. You abandoned me leaving me all alone. I hated you," she concluded. As soon as Tracey mentioned abandonment, it hit Jackson. How many times had he abandoned his wife, Tiffany? Was this a pattern for his previous self? His famous words and actions were of a fool. One thing felt certain, it was time to make sure this former self was buried and stayed that way. He walked over to her and ran his fingers through her hair, brushing it from her face. He was too shocked at his own cruelty to have words, but he gave her his gaze. He looked at her with compassion and acceptance. Now was when he might usually make love to her, but love was never involved or even implied. Jackson now knew that good sex did not mean love. He could tell he only took from this woman in the past. Her body had been his toy and he was clearly a bull in the China shop of her soul. He felt disgusted. As he looked into her, he saw all of her internal scars. Her world was chaotic and had been since childhood. Her father was not abusive, but certainly an absentee alcoholic. She had long ago given up on God or the devil. She did not buy into divine justice, a plan or purpose. Life equated to being born and then dying. The shape of her existence was nothingness.

He asked her to secure her coat. She stood to her feet and did as he asked. Jackson left the room. She knew the drill from the past well. It was time for her to leave she suspected.

When Jackson returned, he had some towels and a bucket of warm water, but she was leaving. He called to her, and she stopped. He walked to the foyer and found her hand on the doorknob. He took her hand with an objective mastery that she found compelling and then led her back to her seat. Her heart raced because he had never pursued her. She had always been desperate for his attention or any validation. The old Jackson was intellectually and emotionally taxing, now she was experiencing a hurricane of feelings. The present was innocent, she felt lost.

"I only wanted you to cover up. I don't have any right to see your body after the man I was to you". He then knelt at her feet, poured the water over them after taking her heels off. He was attentive in a way that threw her into shock at first. Every cell of her body had his attention. She watched in amazement as he washed her feet. The moment was more miraculous than any she had ever experienced. She even considered that this man was not Jackson Riggs, but an imposter. The past was on hold, and she had never been so fully engrossed in a moment. When he dried her feet, he was still so attentive never losing focus or interest. Her eyes were wide, and her mouth hung open. Then he looked up at her, but he did not rise to his feet. He remained her servant. His lips parted and as he spoke her eyes filled with tears. "In old days people wore sandals and traveled mostly by foot. Therefore, their feet were always considered the filthiest part of the body. When one washed the feet of another it was an act of servanthood. Basically, servants serving their masters. Kind of gross, huh?" He smiled and they laughed like children. "There are no holes in your shoes, but I think there may be a big hole in you. A big hole in all of us really." He paused, "I am married, and it appears I have failed two women. I am deeply sorry. On my knees I beg you to forgive me. However, I made a vow that I do not think that I was ever released from. I can't be your romantic, but I will serve and make every reasonable effort to make amends if you allow me."

"I thought you were divorced," she whispered.

"Technically. I suppose that could be true, but even if it is I don't think there is ever a time when we are permitted to stop loving someone, but maybe that is just my foolish mindset."

Her tears were falling, and he found her even more beautiful as she wept. She stayed for nearly an hour mostly in silence. She was coming alive again and it felt like watching a flower bloom in the illusion of speed. He would rise on occasion to wipe her tears away but returned to his knees. He could sense that pain from many years was being released, but he had no idea what the wounds were. Asking about her life and story felt like an intrusion to the cleansing.

"When I woke up this morning, like every morning I felt lonely. Now I am leaving, and I somehow know I won't stay that way."

All she could feel was honesty. It was the very first time she left his home not feeling awful about herself.

Cue the Genesis song, "Throwing It All Away."

CHAPTER 10

The next morning Jackson was sitting on his rooftop. His thoughts started off void as he simply took in the view. Yet, when the sun came up the masses caught his attention. He looked down at the morning traffic wondering about the lives below. He could see so many prim, proper, and pretty people. This was a town of name brands and cars that proclaimed social class. Raleigh was evidently a city of prosperity or maybe these people were just broke on a higher level. People who were not looking for better days. People who had achieved their goals. At least in their minds they had. Logos served as identification, and they drank their coffee from a cup that associated them with sophistication. He wondered if these people had mistaken the shadows for reality. The wealthy of the city shared social status, restaurants, and parties. They paraded as friends, but who would know them in their final minutes. Who would visit when cancer became mean in their own world? Loyalty and friendship only flourish when there is no competition. A bunch of lives trying to outdo the others in positions. It was a disturbing thought to think he had been a leader of this consumer pack. Truth of the matter was that the old Jackson didn't care much about other people. In fact, most of his dealings with others were simply imposing Barry Jenkin's will or his own on the innocent. The question raised its inquiring head again. Who am I? More importantly, who was I?

The steady pace of footsteps grew louder as Jim Adams approached Jackson. There was no need to look over his shoulder because his high-rise condominium was more than adequately protected.

"Good morning, Riggs," Jim announced. "Did you get any sleep last night, sir?"

"I slept for seven weeks, Jim. I am more than well rested," Jackson smiled.

Jim went on to explain that Barry Jenkins had sent him. Jackson's boss was eager to meet with him. It had not been the day Jackson had expected, but he agreed.

Barry Jenkins had earned his law degree from night school. He became an effective ambulance chaser as disability attorneys are often referred. Soon he had offices in Charlotte, Greensboro, Wilmington, and every major market in the state. He was a volatile and innovative attorney, and as his wealth grew, so did his interests. He took pride in contributing to every governor and prominent politician's campaign that he felt served his desires. Almost always, Jenkins' candidate would win their election. Real estate was something that grabbed his attention after reading Donald Trump's, *The Art of the*

Deal. Though Jenkins' face could be seen all over the state on billboards and in commercials, he seldom saw the inside of a courtroom these days. His firm's minions handled that kind of work, and they were a very capable bunch.

He had a clean and uncluttered inner sanctum. His mail, messages and reports had to be displayed on his desk in the most precise and particular manner that Jenkins demanded. Nobody was ever permitted into his office unless summoned by Jenkins. Jackson was seldom seen in the office, but he was never denied Barry's time.

Nothing anyone ever did was good enough for Jenkins. He often unleashed a fiery tongue and lacerating temper. Subordinates often lived in fear of his moods. They were accustomed to anticipating his next angry outburst. Sometimes he could be very charming. He handled power very differently than most people. It was not uncommon for people to be in awe of the man and his complexity.

Jenkins compensated his employees very well, but they were required to give up a substantial part of their lives. It was a trade that most younger associates were easily willing to make fresh out of college and deep in student loan debt. Once on-board, new recruits were encouraged to live a good life, always well above their means. Jenkins realized that high debt for cars, homes, country clubs, vacations, and status essentially enslaved people to his organization. Very few of the staff would want to sacrifice their lifestyle so they churned the wheels of Jenkins' company. Jenkins was a master manipulator.

As fate would have it, Barry Jenkins's office was only a few blocks from Jackson's home. He was perched on the thirty-third floor of the PNC building, Raleigh's tallest. Much like a yachtsman wants a bigger boat, Barry wanted bigger buildings. It bothered him that his hometown didn't have a need for something with ninety-two floors like the Trump Tower. He also owned a summer place in Briarcliff Manor, New York that he used mostly to impress mistresses and potential business partners. His winter home in Palm Beach, Florida was more of his favorite child. That was a home he kept much more secluded but took pride that he had to drive by Trump's mansion often.

When Jackson entered the C.E.O.'s office he was dressed remarkably casual in jeans and a flannel shirt. The older version of him was dressed to kill even when dressed down. The former Jackson wouldn't be caught dead in anything short of Calvin Klein and even that was slumming it. Barry was wearing a sharply tailored suit that cost upwards of four thousand dollars. Jackson's first thought was that the older man with a chipper personality, ruddy face and silvering hair was dressed like a Saudi Prince. Tacky is the word that came to Jackson's mind.

Barry's huge and handcrafted desk was made especially for his office in Pine Hills, North Carolina. However, it was not the only dominant feature of the room. There stood a billiard table near one of the big picture windows and a conference table at the other end of the room. Jackson doubted the pool table was used for anything more than an expression of affluence. Barry had expensive taste, lived in the lap of luxury, and made a point of making his success known. Jackson was taking in the scene gathering information and processing. Once again, he could not see into Barry, and this made Jackson uncomfortable. Why did he see into some people and was blocked so completely from others?

At the first sight of Jackson, Barry rose to his feet. His greeting was very cordial and professional. The two men seemed to search for things to say. However, they now had no past, no memories or common ground. Jackson was never Barry's friend, colleague, or confidant. In fact, although Jackson worked for Barry he wasn't actually on the staff or payroll. Jackson's title was consultant, and he was paid consulting fees. What Barry provided for Jackson was allowances. These allowances paid most of Jackson's bills, but by not being on a salary there were never any real taxes to pay. Every once in a while, a problem or special circumstance would arise, and this is when Barry consulted Jackson. However, this is where the consultation stopped. Jackson offered no advice or service along those lines. Jackson would simply learn of a specific situation and fix the problem according to Barry's desires. How exactly Jackson executed Barry's will was anyone's guess. Ethics and morality never once stood in the way of Jackson's efforts. Both men had a history of slithering their way around any type of law or formality. Now the inconvenient amnesia made the two men complete strangers. Worse yet for Barry was that now the rumors claimed Jackson had become a moral and kind man.

Barry walked over to the wet bar and poured them each a drink. As Barry walked back over, he handed Jackson a rocks glass of straight up Bourbon. It was Michter's 20-year-old Single Barrel Bourbon that cost just under five hundred dollars a bottle.

"I know you don't currently remember, but this was our custom… every time we began a new endeavor, I would pour us both a drink. We would toast as opposed to shaking hands. I am not really sure how that custom came about, but it was definitely ours and I grew fond of it." Of

course, Jackson took the glass and inquired as to what they were drinking. Barry explained that he had been able to impress Jackson with many of the finer things of life over the years. However, Jackson always had his own allegiance to certain things and Bourbon was one. With all his expensive tastes of the past Jackson still slummed it according to Barry drinking Wild Turkey 101, but only Wild Turkey Master's Keep One was in the office wet bar.
"Any particular reason?" Jackson asked.
"Excuse me," Barry didn't understand the question.
"Why had you grown so fond of our custom?"
Barry explained there were two reasons. First, Jackson had never let Barry or Jenkins Enterprises down. In fact, with Jackson on the job no matter the size or significance, the task would be favorably completed. Second, and just as important, was that Barry enjoyed any occasion to break open a bottle of 20-year-old Bourbon. Then Barry asked about the trip to Orlando and wanted to know if Jackson had any memories of it. Barry was more concerned with liability than Jackson's experience. He was well educated on his former employee's condition and memory loss. Jackson countered with a question of his own. He wanted to know why he was in Orlando.

    Jenkins was both confused and fascinated with Jackson's posture and ease. The old Jackson was always coolly withdrawn. Barry's small speeches smacked of explanation and yet little information. Jackson welcomed the familial excess of Barry in hopes of discovering more about the plots of his own life.

Barry walked over to two large leather chairs facing the big windows. Barry took a seat looking out over the city. His actions seemed very deliberate, but he was pondering. "What should I share?" he thought. "How safe is Jackson right now?" He found himself lost in questions and doubt. About a minute later Jackson joined in the next chair. Whereas Barry was racing to keep up with his own thoughts, Jackson was extremely focused. Barry had a glint in his eye that Jackson did not trust. Just how far into evil did Jenkins' political and personal ambitions sink?
"We had a problem with some property we needed or should I say desperately wanted. Some issues needed to be ironed out. I sent you down as the company's ambassador. I must say you did a great job as always. You have a very persuasive way when needed." Jackson pushed for more information, but Barry's doubts resisted. Barry explained that in Jackson's current state it wasn't wise to release information that was as delicate of a matter as insider trading is to the stock market. A deal was on the table thanks to Jackson, but a mountain of paperwork still needed attention. Attorneys needed to

work or fight over details. Jackson understood Barry's stance but was still inquisitive. Whenever it came to people, he had known in the past his mind was blank. However, Jackson felt he did not need to be intuitive to know that Barry Jenkins was not a trustworthy person.

Barry did have ideas and plans to get Jackson back to work. Barry pushed a button and Sal Edwards entered. He was a young wiry looking man fresh out of college. Sal was sharply dressed with a mainstream hipster hairstyle. Jackson was not at all impressed with the pomp and didn't care for Sal immediately. Jackson could sense that he was among wolves. Yet, with their arrogance and influence these wolves did not hide themselves in sheep's clothing. Barry greeted Sal as if he was a proud father.

"Jackson, this man is a real attention getter. His name is Sal and he used to work primarily for you," Barry explained.

Jackson shook Sal's hand.

"What did you do for me?"

Sal went on to explain that there was never a dull moment working for Mr. Riggs. No two workdays had ever been the same. There was never a risk of monotony. Jackson thought to himself that if Sal was any reflection of his older self, then that was just gross.

"Sal is going to show you around… introduce you to people and help you become reacquainted. Then if you are up to it lunch is scheduled with Jeff Kenline later this afternoon at The Capitol Room," Barry explained. Jackson already knew that he was about to hate his day. Yet, his hunger to know who he was drove him to agree very politely.

Jackson followed Sal around the building for over an hour. The tour and introductions were completely boring to him. It was bothersome to Jackson the way Sal would introduce some people and completely overlook others. Sal was young and egotistical. He carried himself with a disturbing pride. Jackson couldn't see inside Sal but felt that he was walking with a very dark personality. Was Sal just young and stupid? Sal certainly wasn't overbearing, but there was something unsettling. Once again when Jackson wanted to see the inside theater of a person's mind, he was blind. The gift would serve others, but never the man who carried the torch. He silently felt aggravation as he realized he could not manipulate, direct or reason with it. His former self was completely self-absorbed, obsessed with his world. He would not have been able to have blind faith. However, now he was a new man. Once again Jackson's peace fell on him, and he trusted in the journey with no worry. The unknown was not scary to Jackson although he felt that he was supposed to be filled with anxiety. Whatever protected Jackson from nervousness was clearly bigger than his own self.

Walking down the hall, Sal was showing off company perks. They had a state-of-the-art gym, restaurants and even childcare. Standing outside of the childcare room, Jackson stopped to look at the toddlers. For the first time since entering the PNC building, he was smiling. He adored their innocence and playfulness. Sal was annoyed that Jackson stopped. Sal had absolutely no interest in children. A woman who had her back to the windows was attending to the most beautiful little boy. He had blonde hair and blue eyes. Jackson loved watching the lady's nurturing nature with the child.

"Beautiful," Jackson almost whispered, but Sal heard.
"Oh yeah, she is smoking hot for sure," Sal said. "You ought to love that chest of hers."
Jackson again was finding Sal to be distasteful.
"And why is that, Sal?" Jackson asked, his tone clearly defining his annoyance.
"Because you bought them," Sal replied giggling.
As Sal was speaking, Tracy Lewan stood up and turned around. Her eyes immediately met Jackson's. It was an unexpected meeting and awkward to say the least. Immediately Jackson was filled with repugnance. This woman is a mother and I treated her like garbage, he

thought. Jackson walked into the nursery. Sal instinctively knew he was not invited and waited on the other side of the picture windows. The young man was unimpressed with this new Jackson, but he still had a very healthy respect for his former boss' self. It was best to obey the weaker version of Jackson before the old one returned. Sal reasoned that the former Jackson would be pleased with his devotion soon enough.

"Is this where you work?"

"No," she answered, "This is my son, Hayden."

The little boy looked up at Jackson with his adorable blue eyes. Knowing that Jackson had not been a good person as his former self, he had to ask.

"Does he like me?"

"He has never met you."

Jackson's thoughts trailed off to his own daughter. He hadn't seen her yet and wondered how she felt about him. If Tracey kept her son away that was a clear indication that he was not good with children. Jackson was not good with people of any age. Jackson looked at Tracey. "I am starting to get the impression that somewhere there is a file on me that reads, 'Does not play well with others'."

Tracey smiled and laughed a little at the irony of the truth. Jackson knelt to Hayden. The two locked eyes. Hayden was shy, but comfortable. The little boy reached to his side and picked up a Mickey Mouse plush doll from the floor. He then offered it to Jackson.

"Who is this?"

"His name is Mickey Mouse, and you can play with him if you want," Hayden spoke so sweetly. Jackson hugged the toy. He then pretended to have Mickey whisper in his ear. "Mickey Mouse says that he likes me just fine but prefers to be with you." Jackson handed the doll to Hayden.

"I am sorry. Me and Mickey have been friends a long time," Hayden explains, taking Mickey back.

"Well, according to Mickey Mouse you are his best friend." Jackson stood back up and Tracey's eyes were soft.

"In the entire three years of his life, he has never offered Mickey to anyone," she offered.

Jackson hugged her. He knew it was time for him to continue with Sal.

He took her hand. "What can I do for you?"

"You are doing just fine," she said softly.

"Tell me something Tracey," Jackson asked. "The man on the other side of that glass. Who is he to me?" Tracey leaned over past his shoulder. She looked over at Sal and grimaced. Jackson studied her face.

"Well," she paused for a long moment "he was your apprentice. He wants to be you." The two laughed. "Not, the current you," she assured Jackson. Again, the two laughed and Jackson assured her that was all the explanation he needed. He kissed her cheek and gave little Hayden a high five. He walked away longing to remain with them.

When Jackson left, Hayden looked up at his mother. "He was a nice man. No, stranger danger?"

She smiled and nodded no.

Cue the Ben Rector song, "Steady Love".

CHAPTER 11

The Capitol Room was clearly where the elite dined. Once inside, many people noticed and recognized Jackson. However, to him they were all strangers. The maître d' greeted Sal and Jackson. "I am sorry, but jackets are required," he pointed out with much reservation. Jackson felt the maître d's uneasiness. He could see inside a stranger again. Jackson's heart pounded with excitement. He realized that his gift had its own agenda but was still present. Jackson was overjoyed and kindly explained that he understood. The maître d' was relieved. Jackson found this to be both entertaining and hysterical. The man went away and returned. "You look to be a 40," the gentleman said, holding up the jacket for Jackson to wear. Jackson was a gentleman and treated him with a kindness unknown to everyone in The Capital Room. The former Jackson was always curt.

"What is your name?"

"Cavazos, Nick Cavazos."

"Thank you, Nick. I appreciate you."

The two men were then led to Jeff Kenline's table. Kenline was a tall man. Even sitting down, he towered over the others beside him. He was the prime specimen of a southern man. With him was George Malley, a long-time advisor and employee of Kenline. The introductions were formal and pleasant. Everyone seemed comfortable but cautious. The Capital Room was a restaurant where Kenline made many of his deals. One might go so far as to recognize the table as his throne room.

Barry Jenkins had organized the lunch with much agenda. He had heard rumors and stories about Jackson knowing things about people just from looking at them. Jenkins was hoping that Jackson would come back revealing secrets about Kenline. However, Jenkins did not realize that Jackson could never use his gift for personal gain.

Sal was quick to get down to business and cut out formalities. "First, I would like to apologize to both of you gentlemen. Today is Jackson's first day back with us after a terrible accident. He has not been briefed on the proposition of your company's sale to the Jenkins organization." Sal had secured Kenline's attention and intensity.

Kenline instantly demurred. "So, Barry has sent me a self-important blowhard. Forgive me Mr. Jackson. I am sorry for your injuries, but this all stinks of bad business. I am not anxious to be the first person you get into bed with, so please tell Barry I am more than disappointed."

Kenline gets up from the table with Malley following his lead. "There is no reason for us to waste each other's time. Bad business will surely lead to bad economics," Kenline says as he places his dinner napkin on the table. The two men begin to leave when Jackson speaks.

"My past indeed works against me, but when all is said and done that is not the man I am. As for the kid, he is a schmuck, Mr. Kenline. Of this there is no doubt, but he is a kid." A suspended hush fell on everyone within earshot. Kenline stopped dead in his tracks and raised his eyebrows looking down at Jackson. "I was reading some magazine in the hospital or maybe at the airport, I forget. It was Fortune or at least something of that genre. In the magazine the writer stated that his father encouraged him to learn golf. Of course, he had very little interest in golf, but his father insisted all good business happens on a golf course. However, you don't play golf do you, Mr. Kenline?" Kenline curiously nodded when he said, "No, I do not."

"And you dine here a lot, don't you Mr. Kenline?"

Jackson wasn't seeing anything; he was guessing everything from a blind perspective. He didn't even know what Kenline's company's business was.

"Yes, as a matter of fact I do," Kenline responded with pride.

"You think Mr. Jenkins is being disrespectful, but I think he sent us here because this is your golf course. I also think he sent me because apparently, I served him well in the past, but let me assure you I have no agenda. I have more pressing matters in my life than this sale. So humbly I suggest that you may want to take your seat. Tell me what you want. Tell me what is important to you. Maybe I am not the man for this job," Jackson pauses, "but maybe I am."

Kenline looked at Jackson and then at Sal. Jackson knew Kenline had a distaste for Sal because he shares it. Jackson was gambling with a combination of brains and instinct. "As for my young friend here, he will sit back and listen to the adults talk." Kenline found that he liked Jackson a lot. His gut told him he was dealing with a sincere man, a feeling he rarely knew in business transactions. Kenline and Malley took their seat. Jackson smiled. "Now Sal will be picking up the tab for this lunch on Mr. Jenkin's dime. I would ask only one thing of you, Mr. Kenline."

"And what is that?" Kenline's face was almost playful but still full of uncertainty. "We are on your turf, so please do us the courtesy of ordering what you think is best off the menu." It was the perfect amount of respect and flattery for Kenline. Kenline pondered for a moment as he studied the menu. He ordered the shrimp and grits because they embodied the spirit of southern hospitality with a New Orleans flare. Shrimp, andouille sausage, mushroom, and onions in a Tasso cream sauce served on top of local stone ground grits. Sal was disgusted, but Jackson was delighted.

The lunch was a huge success. The three men talked about everything under the sun but steered clear of business. Each topic of conversation was a stepping stone toward trust. Kenline seemed fascinated with amnesia and asked Jackson several questions that couldn't be answered. Sal sat quietly and hated every word of the conversation. Sal felt that Jackson was an idiot. He secretly sat there constructing his every word to Barry Jenkins; how he planned to make sure Jackson was never given any responsibility again. He would ruin Jackson's credibility. Sal sat like a pouting child thinking only of how to enrage Barry Jenkins towards Jackson.

The plates were cleared, and coffee was poured. Jackson now felt he had a better idea of the man sitting across from him. Kenline was an older man selling his business. The endeavor was his life's work, and he was now concerned with his legacy. He was wealthy and splurged on life's excesses, but he was not greedy. It was time for Jackson to dive in.

"Mr. Kenline, what is important to you? It's not money. I sense you have got plenty of that. Have your dreams changed? Are you no longer having fun?"

"Tell me this, Jackson. What does Barry intend to do with my company?"

"Profit from it I am sure, just as you have. He is after all a businessman."

"You haven't even asked me what my business is," Kenline inquired.

Jackson was very much aware that he had no idea what Kenline's company manufactured or what service it provided. Instead, Jackson's concentration was on the man.

"No sir, I have no idea."

Kenline grimaced, "Then why are you here? How could you ever manifest this deal?"

"You don't play your cards that close to your chest. You have never really needed to because most of your business deals result from solid relationships. I get that, and I even envy it."

Jackson was clueless to Jenkin's ulterior motives and as a result never lied. "I suspect I am here to learn you," he answered.

Kenline went on to explain that he owned a few hotels off the coast of North Carolina. He owned one on Atlantic

Beach, another on Carolina Beach and a third on Emerald Isle. He had started in the hotel business at the age of fifteen. He would have done anything not to have to work on his father's tobacco farm during the summers. One day he answered an ad in a local paper purely to work out from under the sun. He had held every position in the hotel business as he saved to buy his own. When his father died, a small but significant amount of money was left to him. Enough money to help, but never spoil, his father always insisted. With that he bought his first hotel. At this point in his life, he had bought and sold several. Of course, he dabbled in other business affairs, but the hospitality of a hotel always had his love. Kenline explained that there was heritage in his hotels mixed with his blood, sweat and tears. He detested some of the larger chains and was sure Barry would sell his hotels off to the Hilton or Hyatt. He wanted the people who labored for him to have jobs. He was a very passionate man. It fascinated Kenline that Jackson listened, paid attention, and was even interested. He was no typical businessman. As a result, he was increasingly at ease with Jackson.

"May we go for a short stroll, Mr. Riggs? Just the two of us?"

Outside, Kenline was a little gloomy. The two men walked next to each other. He was about to confess to

Jackson, and he had no idea why. Still, Kenline trusted his instinct.

"Barry has a vice grip on my balls, Mr. Riggs." In a weak moment Jeff Kenline had already signed a contract with Jenkins. He knew he was about to lose his hotels. He would be paid very well, but he felt he had sold his soul. He wanted to know if Jackson could persuade Jenkins to back out of the deal entirely and not kill his legacy. Now Jackson was questioning why he was at the meeting. He obviously wasn't there to secure a sale or get a deal on the table. What did Barry have up his sleeve, Kenline wondered? Jackson placed his hand on Kenline's shoulder and assured him he would investigate things. He made no promises nor declared a plan. Now for the first time Kenline felt at ease. The peace that surpassed his understanding was sweeping over him and he smiled. It was as if this peace that kept overtaking Jackson had now transferred to the other man.

"Why didn't you leave the business to your family?"

"With all my success, I am a failure in many ways. I was obsessed with my work. My family suffered greatly. I have two daughters, both married with children of their own. They have no interest in my hotels. They have no desire to make the sacrifices I did. My wife passed away a few years ago. Our son has been an addict most of his adult life. If I tried to make him CEO of my company, he would lose everything."

The men spoke as friends and that is what Kenline needed most.

Later Sal wore his frustration and anger like a crown. Walking to the car Jackson turned to him. "You know how insurance companies determine medical malpractice rates for doctors?"

Sal was less than interested and just wanted to yell at Jackson. "Bedside manner, kid! All doctors screw up, but people don't tend to sue doctors they like and trust."

Sal's unforgiving eyes displayed his greed, cunning exposition, and most of all, his disdain for the rebuke.

CHAPTER 12

The knock on the door took Autumn away from her homework. She wasn't expecting anyone. She figured it must be something her mother was having delivered. Tiffany was known to be addicted to midnight online shopping sprees, usually buying some old music or books she found on Amazon that were out of print. Her latest find was an old album from an eighties band called The Outfield. She loved their songs, *Your Love* and *Say It Isn't So*. They could leave it at the door, she thought. Then a second knock happened. *This delivery guy is annoying.* Another knock and she was outraged. She went downstairs aggravated and prepared to display all her teenage angst at this guy.

Opening the door to her father was the furthest thing from her mind. Standing there in the flesh, a man who had taken very little interest in her life, just showed up. Immediately she could see a different man in his face. Still, he was a stranger. She had no idea what to say. A part of her wanted to cry. Another part of her felt a nervous kind of excitement. Why was she feeling this flood of emotions?

Jackson stood there looking at his daughter. He had no pictures of her in his apartment and wondered why. She was beautiful. He just took her in like a deep breath. He studied her features. She had his eyes and her mother's lips. She was gorgeous, he kept thinking. The silence was growing uncomfortable for both. *You're the adult here*, he said to himself. *You need to take the lead*, he reasoned.

"Hello. I am your dad," he spoke soft and careful.

"Hey," she returned.

"Where is your mom?"

"Work, I guess." She was standing firm in the doorway, almost like she was guarding her home, but she was much more protective of her heart, whether she knew it or not. *Take it slow*, he kept thinking.

"I am sorry I don't remember you or our relationship," he said.

She assured him it was fine, but of course it was not. He had made being out of her life seem so effortless in days gone by. Still, she had never seen her father act vulnerable before. She could not imagine him ever apologizing to anyone in his life. She was mesmerized to see this person in her father's body. *This is borderline alien-abduction type stuff,* she thought. She was careful with every word that escaped her mouth. She knew he could go away. He had done it before.

"What do you need?" she asked gently.

"My needs are met. I was wondering what I could do for you," he replied.

What the heck kind of answer is that, she wondered.

Jackson excused himself for a moment and walked back to his car. Jim Adams had been watching the entire interaction. Even he was fascinated to see this new incarnation of his old boss. Jackson wanted him to call Tiffany. He wanted an idea of something Autumn enjoyed doing and permission to spend time with her. Jim felt it was an awkward request, but even Jackson's older self always had strange needs and demands.

Once the assignment was given, Jackson ran back up to the door. Just his run seemed playful. Autumn found herself smiling just watching him act like a kid. She could not help but think of him getting hit by a truck. The terrible accident that turned out to be an amazing thing. She knew very little about her father's crash and she wondered what he knew. What she didn't realize was that her father took very little interest in his accident. When he was in Orlando, he was too consumed with seeing into people. He only recently understood that he couldn't see into people he knew.

Politely Jim approached the two.

"What did she say?" Jackson asked with reserved enthusiasm.

"At first, she wasn't too happy you are here while she is working, but after a few choice obscenities, she had an idea," Jim answered.

Jackson turned to Autumn. "Your mom said we can go on an adventure. Would you like that?" Autumn retreated to call her mother. Tiffany had turned into somewhat of a control freak since their divorce. She found it hard to imagine that her mother would agree to an unsupervised outing. It mattered not that the outing was with her father. However, Autumn wanted to go. So, she closed the door leaving her dad and Jim on the porch. She figured her mother might need some convincing or persuading.

Who are these people, Autumn thought as she talked with her mom. Tiffany admitted to being upset at first when Jackson showed up unannounced. However, she felt that Jackson just didn't know any more about certain protocols since his accident. Besides this was proving to be the best version of Jackson she had ever seen. Autumn got a brief lecture, but that was par for the course. The young girl ran upstairs to change her clothes like a typical teenage girl.

Jim Adams drove them to a salon. It hadn't occurred to his daughter to ask where they were going. What was this adventure that lay ahead? All her big brown eyes could do was look at her father. He was participating in this game called her life. She had butterflies.

They got out of the car. "Your mom says you love manicures, do you mind?"

"When I mind, you will know I mind."

Inside they went.

He didn't feel silly sitting next to her having his own hands massaged. It was worth it. The conversation they shared was still small. Autumn remained shy, surprised, and speechless. However, it was evident she was enjoying herself and she was especially enjoying her father.

"What are you made of?

"You mean besides the sperm and egg you and Tiffany provided?"

Jackson was at a loss for words for the first time since his awakening.

"The Breakfast Club, Ferris Bueller's Day off, Say Anything."

Jackson said nothing.

"You don't remember motion pictures?"

Jackson grimaced and nodded no.

"When I was a kid, every Monday night was eighties night. You introduced me to all the old and good stuff. In a way, you ruined modern movies for me."

"When did that stop?"

"When you stopped making stars," she rather enjoyed being the teacher.

"You always made my sandwiches and French toast in star shapes. I knew when you stopped, everything would change."

She had not intended on being that deep, but her feelings and thoughts had been near the surface for years.

"What was your favorite movie?"

Autumn shrugged her shoulders. She didn't really know.

Afterwards they went shopping at Macy's. He insisted she choose the dress that made her feel most beautiful. She started to look around cautiously. Her eyes drifted to the price tags. She felt out of place. Jackson encouraged her to get whatever she wanted. His voice was soft. Who was this strange man showering her with the attention of a loving father? When he observed her looking at price tags, he gently took the tag from her hand. "You buy the dress you want." Her big brown eyes looked up at him in disbelief. It felt like she had tried on dozens of dresses, but her face showed so much excitement. She finally settled on a perfect red dress. He had set his sights on finding a way to her heart. His attention was completely on her. He was not thinking of Barry Jenkins, his condition, or even Tiffany. He had learned to live in the moment and focus on whom he was with. The old Jackson would have been impatient living in the future, eager to move onto his next task. He had never been so relaxed. She felt like Julia Roberts in *Pretty Woman* when Richard Gere takes her shopping.

"Now go get some shoes to go with that beautiful dress. I need to make a quick call." Jackson handed the dress to Jim and walked away from the two. He dialed Jeff Kenline. When Kenline answered, Jackson explained that he was on a special date with his daughter. Was it possible for Mr. Kenline to get a reservation for two at The Capitol Room? The request was very well received. Jackson knew Kenline had the clout to get them a table without a reservation or long wait.

CHAPTER 13

On the way to dinner, they stopped at his condo. His daughter had never been to his home before. She was amazed at how her dad lived. She had no idea he thought his place was pretentious and void of warmth. He had no idea she felt the same way. Autumn put on her new dress and Jackson put a on a jacket and tie. He felt uncomfortable in his old clothes. He didn't see himself as a business attire kind of guy. She came out of the spare bedroom to meet him in the living room. He stood there feeling like a love-struck adolescent. He adored his daughter, and her beauty was captivating. Once again, he could see her mother in her which was exhilarating. He wondered what gestures and mannerisms they shared. He reached his hand out to hers and then led her to the car. They didn't speak for a few minutes. Autumn wasn't afraid of silence, something she inherited from her dad. They both relished in the moment.

"*The Never-Ending Story.*"

He was lost.

"My favorite movie."

At The Capital Room, Mr. Kenline had made sure a table was waiting to overlook the beautiful night grounds. It was a truly breath-taking view. The reflection of stars and nearby lights glimmered on the nearby lake. The waiter approached the table.

"Welcome. Tonight, our chef has prepared a vegetarian lentil and pumpkin soup." The server was explaining the specials, but Jackson was distracted. He could see into the young man. He could see his fear, his concern and more deeply a dejected past. *Not now,* he thought. Jackson was fully engaged in his daughter.

"Excuse me," Jackson interrupted. "Would you be so kind as to get me your manager?" He spoke kindly, but he never lost that air of authority.

The request was unsettling. Jackson could see the waiter wondering if he had done something wrong. As he walked away from their table Autumn asked Jackson what that was about.

"Would you mind terribly if Sam joined us for dinner this evening, honey?" Jackson asked.

"Sam?"

"Our server," he replied, but before he could explain, Sam had returned with the manager.

"Good evening, sir. How may I be of service to you?" The manager asked.

Jackson stood up and shook his hand. "Mr. Kenline was very clear that this evening's dining should be beyond a pristine experience," the manager said.

"That is very gracious of both you and Mr. Kenline. Look, I have somewhat of an unorthodox request this evening."

"What might that be, sir?"

"I would like to request the company of Sam this evening to dine with us."

Sam and the manager looked at each other with wide-eyed surprise.

"You don't appear to be that busy this evening. I know you have those special little jackets in a coat room. Jackson never took his gaze off the manager. He knew that the request was odd, but he needed to help Sam find clarity. He could also sense the manager searching for a logical reason to decline the offer. So, Jackson took to dropping Mr. Kenline's name as some extra persuasion. It was a clumsy power play but provided the collaboration Jackson wanted. The manager turned to Sam the server and gave a nod of approval. Jackson then pulled out a chair for Sam. Autumn was speechless. Who does something like what her dad just did? As a teenager, she still embarrassed easily. Then it struck her. She just thought of him as her dad and not a random distant father. She had no need to reduce him to a sperm donor as she had in the past. Maybe her healing had begun? Panic had befallen on her. When might the father of her past return? He doesn't even really know me, she realized. What if he doesn't like me? Anxiety

was defeating her joy. Jackson looked at his girl and could see her angst. He reached over and laid his hand on hers. He said nothing. Once again, through touch, Jackson's peace transferred to his daughter's heart, mind, and soul.
"The battlefield is always in the mind, honey."
She felt peace wash over her. In a way she was freaked out, but she soon realized she could just relax.

Now they were studying the menu. Autumn took note of two things. One, there were no prices, and two, she had no idea what most of the items were. The selections included Masa Toro with Caviar, Shirasu, and Pigeon with warm foie gras sorbet. Jackson looked over at his daughter. He could immediately see her frustration with the complexity of the menu. It was cute, he thought. Jackson took no joy in her confusion, but only he realized that most of the patrons were as clueless as his little girl. He looked over at Sam who had his face buried in the menu. Sam glanced up. "Sam, how is the Kobe and Matsusaka Steak?" Sam's face lit up as he explained it was the favorite dish on the menu. Jackson paused for a moment and then looked at his daughter with an awkward uncertainty. "Honey, aren't you a vegetarian?'
"No!" Autumn replied. Jackson took the lead and ordered. Just before the new server stepped away from the table Jackson spoke up one more time.

"And cheese sticks. Three orders please, to start with."

They ate and enjoyed the meal. Sam was more comfortable because Jackson kept the conversation fun and light. He had lots of questions for both Sam and his daughter. Autumn took a friendly liking to Sam much easier than she expected. Even their differences were fun. Jackson had asked what Sam's favorite motion pictures were. Autumn tried to correct her dad and say they are just called movies, but he would have no part of it. Autumn declared *The Princess Bride*, (she had forgotten to mention), was the best movie of all time. While Sam's choices were the original Star Wars trilogy, the first two Godfathers or anything Monty Python. A fun-spirited debate ensued. Sam would occasionally see his manager glancing over at their table. Jackson thought it was funny that his daughter's choice had changed several times that evening.

"Now Sam," Jackson's demeanor changed. He came across more stoic now. "I sense the fatherless void you are feeling. I want to assure you. Your father loves you. The split between him and your mother was very vicious. She moved you here before you were even born. She also made every attempt to keep him out of your life. Now pay attention... I am not implying your mother is a bad person. She simply did what she felt was right. People tend to do what they think is right in their own hearts, but sadly the heart can be very misleading. On your third birthday, your father started writing in a journal to you. He has kept it up all these years. He even wrote to you last night," Jackson offered.

Sam's face was a mix of shock and awe. He was not expecting this conversation. Sheepishly he asked how Jackson knew his father. But of course, Jackson did not. Jackson went on to explain this was the very reason he had asked Sam to join them at the table. Autumn sat silently as if she were watching a movie. Her father was bringing tears to a grown man's eyes, even though he was still a very young man. Jackson was being kind on a level that she could not measure. All the sudden, Sam was so much more than just an intrusion as she initially thought. He was no longer just a fun and casual dinner companion. He was a guy on a journey with a story. It fascinated her that her dad just jumped right into his heart and soul. "You know your father's name. I know you look at his social media pages. He has never set his setting to private in hopes you would look for him. He doesn't know how to approach you. However, Sam, he does love you. His heart has been broken just as you have. I am not saying anything he did was right, but he has lived life as a defeated man for years. The battle that enraged between your mother, her family and your dad simply wore him out. Tonight, you should send him a message."

"What would I even say?" Sam asked.

Sam's affection for his father superseded the emotional bruises sustained over the years.

"Almost every relationship starts off between two strangers. Most greetings are remarkably simple. Just say hey, and you will see the floodgates of conversation open."

Sam's arms went limp, his thoughts scattering yet slowly coming together because the peace of Jackson was contagious. He stood up from the table. Jackson rose to meet him. Autumn watched her father hug a stranger. It wasn't one of those superficial hugs. It was an embrace. Jackson held onto Sam. It was a nurturing kind of embrace and the peace that Jackson knew now settled on Sam.

"Now go and let the healing begin but be patient with it. Remember peace is not freedom from life's storms, but rather finding serenity in the storm. That takes courage; a courage most won't understand." Jackson spoke softer now.

On the ride home Autumn was silent. She was fixated on the night's events. Jackson chose to let the silence be and not force anything. His days of needing to be in control of all matters were over. His new self-understood control on any level was an illusion. He had no idea what his daughter was thinking. Still, he considered their night to be a success.

As he walked her up to the front door Autumn broke her silence.

"How did you know those things about that guy?"

"I don't know. Sometimes I just see people and it is like they are thinking out loud. I can hear their thoughts. Sometimes I see pictures."

"Then what am I thinking?" she asked nervously.

When he confessed, he had no idea she was relieved. She had been worried that he could see into her mind, her heart, and her soul...a thought no teenager welcomes about their parents.

"Autumn, I can never see into people for any self-serving reason. I don't know why, but that just seems to be how this gift works. It is far from indulgence, that is for sure."

She was extremely comforted by that. He explained that just maybe when there is no agenda his mind's eye has a clearer view. Maybe everybody has this gift, but they just grow up and grow out of it.

"I've changed my mind; my favorite movie is *Grease* and that is my final answer."

Jackson laughed, "Why *Grease*?"

"Because it is your favorite."

Concrete information about his past felt nice. Once again, he felt like a boy in men's clothing.

Cue the Bruce Springsteen song, "The Nothing Man."

Upstairs Tiffany had heard the car pull up. She considered going down to meet him. In fact, the entire evening she had wrestled with what she might do when they arrived home. There was a significant place of her heart that did want to see him. It was a special place inside of her that she feared and adored. She was so very anxious to see if this time would be different. However, she decided this was a daddy daughter night. She would stay away.

Autumn closed the door behind her and walked up the stairs. She knew her mother was awake with anticipation. She smiled like she had been on a first date. When she opened her mother's door Tiffany was pretending to read a book, but she had not read a page all evening. Her performance was miserable. Tiffany's heart warmed when she saw her little girl's face full of joy. The two just embraced.

"How are you feeling, honey?"

Autumn paused. The long silence was almost disturbing. Long silences seemed to be very fashionable lately. Tiffany's comfort still came from her daughter's expression. She started to reply a few times but bridled her tongue. From Autumn's vantage point she knew it was time to be a little vague.

"I have been angry at him for years. I convinced myself he was just my sperm donor, but tonight I think I am sure of two things. One, the hurt hasn't gone away, but two, it is not the same, mom." Tiffany was blown away at her daughter's depth of expression. She was looking for avenues to examine Jackson's motivation, but the view was blurred.

"You know how sometimes a person will look at you. In an instant you feel like their eyes just look right into you. Well, when I was with my dad it feels like he is looking into everyone like that. Yet, he still managed to make me feel like all his attention was on me. He invited the waiter to sit and eat with us. I wanted to be offended, mad, jealous, but it all felt so natural in a world's gone crazy kind of way."

"I like your new dad too, but we need to be careful. Things have a way of changing."

"The thing is my old dad never knew this man he has become. If his memory comes back, he will then know both versions. There is no way he could ever go back to his former self."

    Cue the Need to Breathe song, "Into the Mystery."

CHAPTER 14

The following morning Jackson Riggs entered the PNC building where Barry Jenkins offices resided with gumption. He was feeling more confident today. He was finally settled, and peace prevailed inside of him.

Barry Jenkins had spent the morning reviewing the state's gubernatorial campaign polls and numbers. Barry had a horse in this race. Scot Clemons had been a cash cow attorney for the firm. He had been fiercely loyal to everything Jenkins. With Clemons as Governor, Barry's power and influence were sure to grow and benefit in multiple ways. However, the corporate lawyer was trailing behind the republican candidate. Barry didn't like to lose nor did he like his team
to lose. John Edwards became a North Carolina senator and even presidential candidate birthed out of a successful law practice. Barry knew the odds were not against Clemons. Unlike Edwards, Clemons was not at risk of a National Enquirer expose'.

On a coffee table was a bowl of shredded fifty-dollar bills. Although his office had works from Picasso, Pollock, and local artists, the dish of torn money always commanded people's attention. Barry was known to invite people to throw money in as a way of cementing collaborations. Oddly, the practice proved to create camaraderie. The benefits of power were lovely, Barry felt, and the dish of money expressed the sentiment.

Barry's advisors were sitting with him. The men were often referred to as the three wise men. These men weren't just brilliant, they were masters at manipulating situations. In fact, their ideas had sent the old Jackson on many unethical missions. Today their brainstorming was coming up void. They tried several attempts to discredit the republican candidate, but he was proving to be Teflon. Nothing would stick to the man. The room fell silent as ideas went mute.

Barry slammed his fist on a desk and yelled, "I will be damned if I am going to let these old southern republicans steal the governor's influence from me! Those people think this is the Bible belt, but it is not! It is the Bible hang man's noose! This can't happen gentlemen!" Barry's voice was a growl. The men's eyes were cold. For the first time Barry was on the ropes in what was about to be the final round.

Unexpectedly, one of the wise men spoke up. His voice did more than break the silence, it broke the tension as well.

"That is it," he spoke confidently in his revelation. "There is an old guard of republicans that are voting. We need to attract the younger voters. The liberal-minded."

"There are a lot of small towns in this state full of young people that pay no attention to elections," Barry countered.

The wise man explained that Barry had a point, but a limited one. The college towns and metropolitan areas of the state had a lot of young people that did campaign and vote for candidates. The problem this election year was there were no issues of interest to the younger voters. They needed a way to lure the younger people to their party's side, not behind a candidate, but rather an issue. Then these young people would just vote the party line and be in and out of the voter's booth in seconds.

Barry was engrossed in this proposal that was about to prove to be insanely excellent. The wise man proposed they put marijuana on the ballot. They needed to spearhead a campaign to legalize marijuana. Barry sat back in his chair. The idea was fresh and would need a lot of tweaking, but superb. An idea that would cost Barry lots of money but win him a governorship.

The interruption was unexpected and unwelcome. Jackson simply walked past Jenkins's secretary. She was normally very good at being a gatekeeper. The three wise men flipped around in their chairs as if they had been caught red-handed in one of their schemes. Barry wore the intruder's frustration on his face. Jackson only studied their faces and was unphased by the men.

"Good morning," Jackson announced. Although he appeared unaware of his interruption, but he knew exactly what he was doing. He just didn't care.

"Mr. Jenkins, with all due respect, I took the liberty of firing Sal." The three wise men's eyes diverted from one man's announcement to Jenkins' response. Barry Jenkins was a man with an unquenchable appetite for control. Jackson's action was offensive to all of Barry's senses. Barry remained remarkably calm considering the morning he was having. He simply asked Jackson to explain the action.

"He is unlikable," was all Jackson offered. To Barry these were business decisions not personal preferences.

"So, you are ready to venture out on your own? You see no need for an experienced navigator?" Barry was annoyed. Yet, he had no idea how heightened his annoyance would become.

Barry's phone buzzed. His secretary was a seasoned professional and she knew the strict rules Barry enforced. If she was buzzing in during a meeting with the three wise men, her matter must be of an urgent and very important nature. He once explained to her that death was not an emergency. He could do nothing for the dead. If he needed to be notified of a death it should be at a most opportune time, but never interrupt his affairs. He took a deep breath and answered the phone.

"Mr. Jenkins, there is a Rosemary Appleman here," the secretary stated. Of course, Jenkins had no idea who or what a Rosemary Appleman was. He demanded to know her business with him. Jackson and the three wise men watched Barry mildly erupt like a cartoon volcano. The secretary paused and Barry fumed.

"She is here at Mr. Riggs request. Apparently, she works for us now."

Barry forced his shoulders back; his tension was showing. *I should have known,* he thought. A softer, but agitated voice said to send her in. The three wise men looked spaced out.

Then entered Rosemary Appleman. The older lady was full of energy and wore a huge smile. She walked in without any intimidation or shyness. She had never met a stranger. She handed Jackson some files he had asked for. She then proceeded to introduce herself to all three of the wise men.

"Anyone ever tell you boys you look like them men from *The Matrix*? You know the men all dressed in black?" The three wise men didn't smile or answer. "Hmm. You kind of act like them too." She extended her hand to Barry Jenkins.

"You must be the big boss. Mighty fine to meet you, sir." Barry stared at her face. He saw no pride, no disgrace, no fear, no hate, just a joy-filled woman in her early seventies. She was childlike. She was harmless he thought. If this is whom Jackson wants as a sidekick, then fine. For the first time he felt like something was going his way. Nothing about Rosemary was a threat.

"Tell me," he asked smiling, "how exactly do you know Mr. Riggs?" Barry always exercised jurisdiction over chance and ignorance. His questions always came across as demands. Rosemary grimaced. "You know Mr. Jenkins; Jackson absolutely does not like to be addressed so formerly. He prefers a first name basis. Nicknames are fine too, but none of this mister business." Barry was amused. She kept proving to be a very simple woman. Rosemary then explained she was his nurse. She was there when he opened his eyes. She was there to witness all the miracles too…his immediate full body function and how he saw things about people, people he had never met.
Barry gestured for her to take a seat. The wise men's eyes followed her just like the men from *The Matrix*. She sat and looked back at the men with an uncertain glare. "What was the bad man's name in that Matrix movie anyway?" she asked so innocently.

Barry Jenkins explained that *The Matrix* was one of his favorite movie trilogies second only to *The Godfather*. "The main antagonist was Agent Smith."

"You must really like that motion picture Mr. Jenkins, because you've got yourself three Agent Smiths over there."

Jackson controlled his amusement.

"What did you give Jackson just now?"

"The contracts he asked for...a deal you have brewing with Jeff Kenline. That was his first order of business for me," she answered so innocently.

Barry asked where she got a hold of such confidential information. "From the contracts office a few floors below." She went on to explain that Jackson wanted to review them first thing. Barry had two competing thoughts. First, how was she able to access that information so easily? Second, maybe he was underestimating this woman. Was she some sort of sleuth that simply pretended to be foolish much like the old TV detective Colombo?

"Yes sir, you are buying three properties from Mr. Kenline. There is one on Atlantic Beach, another on Carolina Beach and a third on Emerald Isle".

Barry looked to the three wise men. "Agent Smiths, if you will get to work on what we were discussing. It looks like I might be tied up here for a bit. You're excused." Barry spoke with his authority. As they left Jackson took a seat.

"Please explain to me how you were able to get your hands on those contracts?" Barry was investigating. Was there a security breach? Was his staff just that unprofessional? How many incompetent idiots were losing their jobs today he wondered in rage? Rosemary explained she simply went to the contract's office, dropped Jackson's name and immediately everyone was so helpful, kind and expedient. Suddenly it occurred to Barry, he had never made it widely known to limit Jackson's access or reach in the organization. In the past Jackson Riggs had every inch of the organization's resources at his beckon call. If anyone denied Jackson access to anything it would cost jobs. This was a widely understood rule. Nothing was out of Jackson's reach because he always had Barry's interest and desires as his objective. Now everything had changed. Jackson was a new and unimproved man in Barry's eyes. However, Barry remained confident that his amnesia would wear off and the old Jackson would return.

"Why are you in need of the contracts?" Barry's gaze was squarely on Jackson. "To read them, naturally." Jackson's reply was simple. It bugged Barry that the new Jackson had nothing to prove. Both versions of Jackson were not easily intimidated. Yet, the old version never once gave Barry reason to worry. The old Jackson was respectful even with his few words and lack of emotion. Barry did not like the thought of Jackson now standing on moral ground.

"You want something from me regarding this deal with Kenline, but I don't yet know what that is. I need to understand the deal."

"I want to know what you learned about Kenline," Barry replied, but what he really wanted was secrets. He was hoping that Jackson saw into the man's soul. Subtly, Barry asked if there was anything worth sharing about Kenline. Jackson realized what Barry was seeking. Suddenly it was clear as if a light bulb had lit. "He feels he made this sale under duress. He doesn't want it. He fears you are going to do something with his hotels that will kill his legacy. Kenline has heard a rumor of another sale that is unsettling".

Barry smiled; his lips curling a bit like the Grinch. "You could see all of that?" Jackson explained no. He saw nothing into the man. Barry was confused. "We went for a walk, and he told me."

Barry was frustrated. He could hear the blood in his veins rush and feel his blood pressure rise. "Why would anyone in business crawl into a deal that wasn't potentially profitable? Of course, I am working a deal. I plan to sell those properties to the Cherokee, and they will turn them into Casinos."

"Will the people of North Carolina even go for that?" Jackson inquired.

Barry assured his audience that for years he was told the state would never introduce the lottery, but they had. As a result, with the right man as governor, he was certain Casinos could be introduced to the coastline. What Barry didn't explain was that he would retain a secret partnership with his Cherokee businessmen. Barry had the potential and promise of pocketing millions.

"He doesn't want any of that," Jackson somberly replied. "Too bad! That contract is solid, and the ink of his signature is dry. It is happening and there in nothing Jeff Kenline and his moral guilt trip can do about it."

Jackson rose to his feet and Rosemary followed. "Then let me know when you have something else for us to take care of for you." That was all the courtesy Jackson afforded Barry before he left the office.

Outside of the office Jackson caught his reflection in a window. He stared at himself. He still didn't know his own face. He still had no idea who he once was. How cruel and cold had his former self been? Had this old self truly vanished or was he lurking beneath the surface? How many people had he wounded in heartless deals and corporate battles of the past? He hated not knowing. Then just as worry was about to overtake him that familiar peace visited once again. Stress was clearly not welcome in the new Jackson Riggs.

Rosemary approached him slowly. She put her hand on his shoulder. A version of Jackson feeling disturbed was unfamiliar to her. He turned to her. "Take the contracts and start reviewing them. I want every letter and punctuation mark reviewed," he explained to her. He knew in his heart there was something wrong with the deal, an error that would be in his favor, but he had no idea what.

"Why don't we have an attorney look at this? They are much more qualified than I am," Rosemary offered.

"If spending time in this building has taught me anything, it has showed me that attorneys are not to be trusted." She instinctively knew not to argue her point with him. He knew her lack of legal training would afford her an unusual insight. She would not amputate sections of the documents some others might and thus miss the revelation.

Chapter 15

Jim Adams was waiting for Jackson who wanted to be taken to Tiffany's home. It would be an unexpected house call, but he wasn't concerned. Tiffany was a woman that thrived on order in her life. She made lists, kept calendars, and even scheduled her down time. Spontaneity was not her strength, or a joy, nor did she intend it to be. On the drive over Jackson had two things on his mind. One, what was missing in the contracts that would be to their advantage. He was so certain it was there that he wasn't even worried. His mind was working more like trying to solve a puzzle. Two, why was he in Orlando? This nagged at him like an itch he couldn't reach.

They pulled up in front of Tiffany's house. Normally Jim would wait outside, never sure how long the visit might last.
"I am going to need you to do me a favor," Jackson said.
In the past Jim resented running errands for Jackson because of his distaste for the man. Nowadays he was as enthusiastic as a child helping a parent. Jim looked back at Jackson.
"Sidewalk chalk? I need that."
Jackson squeaked out a minor smile. He could sense Jim's sense of confusion. Jim felt he needed clarification.

"You got it right," Jackson assured him. Jackson wanted Jim to go purchase a few boxes of sidewalk chalk. Getting out of the car Jackson looked backed and enjoyed Jim's lost expression.

Jackson waited at the front door. He would get butterflies every time he rang the doorbell of his ex-wife and daughter. He simply adored every line in their faces, their posture, their eyes, and the sound of their voices. He was smitten with his family. After all he reasoned a broken family is still a family none-the-less.

Autumn answered and she immediately hugged her dad. It was the first time she had done such a thing in years. Just a few weeks ago she was making peace with his death and now she was in his arms. While most kids her age were learning of hot new bands or movie stars, fashion trends, or new apps, she was discovering her dad. When she pulled away, she smiled at him, but tucked her hair behind her ears in a cute teenager kind of manner. Her enthusiastic smile began to melt into an awkward one. Jackson remained silent. He never wanted to pressure Autumn in any way to accept him. He simply wanted to win her heart. What he didn't know was he already had.

Tiffany came around the corner, her face like a deer caught in head lights. She was dressed in a black dress that complimented her every feature. Jackson stepped into the foyer from the porch. Something was stirring as if the two had just lived a month of dreaded Mondays. Then the shocking Tsunami hit. Steve Andrews walked around the corner. The two men's eyes met, and the silence was deafening. Steve was a picture of GQ that had just come to life. Everything about his presence was visually perfect. Now Jackson understood the awkwardness. Autumn and Tiffany exchanged glances, their eyes shooting around the room like broken arrows. Tiffany was in her worst place, an environment that she did not control. She told herself to just breathe in and out. "My name is Jackson Riggs," he said approaching Steve cordially, as if at a business meeting. Tiffany's heart raced. Memories of a rude and ruthless ex-husband haunted her. The vintage version of Jackson would have shown no emotion. He would be cutting and coy. He would gaze on Steve as a predator would. Steve offered an equally pleasant greeting and then looked to Tiffany for direction. Steve knew very little about the new version of Jackson. And he certainly did not know that feelings were rising in Tiffany for her ex-husband.

"I see I caught you at a bad time. I apologize for the intrusion. I was just in the neighborhood. Well, that is kind of a lie," he conceded as he smiled flirtatiously. "Forgive me. What are we up to tonight?" Jackson kept a soft stare in Steve's direction.

Tiffany stepped in and explained that she and Steve had plans. She knew immediately that no version of Jackson would accept vague answers. As she spoke, she monitored her ex-husband's every move. Jackson only listened and followed what was happening. His face gave them no indication of his thoughts or intentions. He was once a man with an explosive temper. Steve had heard stories and was clearly on the defensive. The weight of a former Jackson was too much to take on. Autumn found the interactions entertaining. She had relaxed. She may not know how her dad would react, but she knew it would be unlike anything anyone expected. Suddenly it occurred to Jackson that Tiffany was anticipating an eruption. A slight smile crept on his face, but just how notorious was this grin. Autumn tried to contain her giggle, but she could see her father studying Steve. She knew that this meant her dad was reading this man's mail.

"Well, I don't want to intrude. Have a lovely evening." Jackson nodded, turned, and began out the door. Tiffany wasn't certain she was thrilled to see him leave but was glad the suspense was over. Autumn was disappointed. She expected her father to do something unusual whatever that was. In just one day, his daughter had learned to expect the unexpected. Steve smiled at Tiffany as if they had all dodged a bullet. However, just when everyone thought it was safe to exhale Jackson turned back around.

"Steve, may I see you outside for just a minute?"

Autumn smiled a huge smile. This is what she had stuck around for.

Steve stepped outside. Jackson reached behind him and pulled the door closed. Steve was uneasy. He had heard stories about Jackson and none of them good. Tiffany had rejected everything about her ex-husband while Steve had known her.

"What are you doing Steve?" Jackson asked in the most matter of fact way. However, Jackson wasn't attacking Steve.

Inside both Autumn and Tiffany were taking turns looking through the peep hole.

"Look I know she is your ex-wife," Steve tried to offer, but Jackson cut him off. Jackson asked the question again. Every word the same, but the tone was softer and safer for Steve this time. Steve felt more confused than ever. The words made for a simple question, but the answer seemed deeper. Steve began to speak again. He tried to offer the evening's agenda, but again Jackson insisted they let go of mediocrity.

Jackson was intruding upon Steve's personal space.
Inside Tiffany reached for the doorknob, but Autumn grabbed her mother's hand. The two looked at each other. For the first time in their lives, Autumn was taking control. Tiffany stared at her daughter feeling offended and proud at the same time. What was happening in this world and life of hers? Autumn offered her mother a comforting look very similar to what she had seen in her father. Slowly Tiffany's eye returned to the peep hole.

Jackson looked into Steve's eyes. Steve was naturally uncomfortable.

"Where love and loss meet are a most painful place to be," Jackson said.

He then let his words soak in with a few moments of silence. Steve was beginning to have an unfamiliar vulnerable feeling. A wind blew that felt a lot colder than usual.

"You are self-medicating, and you want to use my family to do it," Jackson was speaking with the authority of a father. Jackson basically told Steve his own story, which was a short story since Jackson's memory was very limited. Steve had only been separated from his wife for nine months. When Jackson pointed this out Steve almost went into shock. *How could this man know details of my life?*

Steve wondered. He felt his heart race faster and emotions rise.

Inside Tiffany's mouth fell open as she witnessed whatever it was, she was seeing. Her ex-husband seemed to be counseling this man. Furthermore, in mere minutes Jackson seemed to be a wrecking ball to Steve's walls. Tiffany could see Steve's body language change. Steve's head was slightly tilted, and he was listening keenly to Jackson. His posture was more relaxed, Tiffany observed. Autumn watched her mom. She didn't dare try and take over the peep hole. She knew her mother was seeing first-hand what she would never have been able to articulate.

"I have made so many mistakes," Steve confessed.

"A mistake is when you accidentally spill a glass of milk. You sir made choices. You were able to choose your action, but never the consequences. Now you are unhappy with the result. It is up to you to offer restitution to those you have hurt." Jackson was always firm and yet gentle. He spoke in a manner of explaining and never judging. Steve stood still unsure of himself. His thoughts were deep. Jackson allowed for a perfect amount of silence before his final words. "You are not the only one in your situation who is hurting."

Inside Tiffany's eyes were wide with awe. Autumn had transitioned to sitting on the stairs.

Steve's mind had already been ambushed and Jackson had only just begun.

"I realize the embezzlement from the insurance company in Chicago was years ago. I also know the money is long gone, but you will never be free. Free from the guilt. Free from the secret until you go back and tell them what you did."

"But I could go to jail."

"Which is worse? Jail or the internal prison you are already living in? Remember the right thing doesn't have to be easy, but it does the body good."

It felt good to Steve that someone else knew his secret. He didn't feel comfortable with the idea of coming clean, but he did enjoy the transparency Jackson provided.

Steve walked away no longer a defeated man, but on a road to redemption. For the first time in his life, he had a chance to be a man of integrity. Part of his soul felt like it had been kicked to the ground and the other part felt lifted. He was a man of transformation. It was anyone's guess what that might look like in a year.

"I am learning that what is seen isn't necessarily true. It can be as misleading as a desert mirage. We don't need to pretend or wear masks, but we do. This is your chance to be free from all of that. I wish you the best."

Steve simply walked down the steps and away from the house, his mind completely void of Tiffany.

Cue the Alec Benjamin song, "Devil Doesn't Bargain."

Jackson opened the door. His mood completely changed. He was now with his family. Jackson said absolutely nothing about Steve's situation. The new Jackson simply did not share the dirty laundry of other people for gossip. Tiffany looked at her ex-husband as if a tiger had just entered her house.

"I have a question. Was there anything my former self was particularly bad doing? What would I make a fool out of myself trying to do?"

"Being a dad," Autumn said and the two laughed.

"I think the three of us should make a night of it," Jackson announced. On any other day that might seem like a reasonable idea, but not today.

Tiffany was still in transitional shock. She began to huff and puff. There was nothing to be angry about. Honestly, she wasn't looking forward to an evening with Steve anyway. Yet, every fiber of her being was screaming that she was living in a crazy world. Had her present-day existence with Jackson become the new normal? One thing for sure was that she had no control. Things were hardly spiraling out of control, but that is all she felt. Tiffany's preconceived notions about her world were drowning.

She erupted. Her voice was barely below a roar. Her words made no sense as she chastised Jackson or the situation or both. The words just kept pouring out. She simply had no idea what she was trying to say because she didn't understand her own feelings. She was yelling with her hands almost like a conductor of a symphony. Her arms collapsed and she retreated upstairs.

Jackson took a seat on the stairs next to Autumn. Slowly Autumn looked up at her dad. "It's funny, that means she likes it," Autumn offered her dad. "Falling apart is the only way for her to change. Nothing can be rebuilt that isn't torn down."

Jackson turned to his daughter. He wanted to worry about Tiffany, but that intrusive peace kept taking over. Now his daughter was speaking wisdom. He head-locked hugged her. "I guess this is a *What About Bob* moment," he said. She gave him her inquisitive puppy dog eyes. "It is an old movie with Bill Murray and Richard Dreyfuss. In the motion picture the Dreyfuss Character has written a book called *Baby Steps*. So that is what I am thinking in relation to your mom. Baby steps." Jackson explained.

Autumn pulled away. She looked at her father with wonder. "You remember a movie?" she questioned. The observation surprised even him. He took in the revelation. He looked at his hands and he was calm – much calmer than he expected he would be. Maybe there was a part of him that he could know once more. Maybe there was some light in his old self. Maybe he really was much darker than even he realized. Was his soul about to tell him his own secrets? He started to walk into anxiety, but the rush of peace once again intruded. *Who was I?* He was thrilled at the prospect of hope.

He looked at Autumn and asked what she was thinking. She was scared that if his memory came back so would his old self. He assured his beloved daughter that he loved her more than he ever had anything or anyone apart from Tiffany. He wasn't going back to his former self no matter the situation. He was setting things right and they were not going to go wrong. In the past what he said and what he meant always seemed to disagree. However, now his words and intentions had formed an alliance. He was going to be there for her always. He was never going to make her cry again. What was more amazing than his words or actions is that she believed him. She knew she had a father.

"This is a muffin man moment."

"A what?"

"When I was little, I loved the song *The Muffin Man*. You used to dance with me and play that song. When you looked at me, I knew you loved me. This is a Muffin Man moment."

"I like it."

The later part of the night had slid into place. Tiffany was still upstairs. She was silent. Feelings inside her were stirring a new light. She hadn't simply lost control of her surroundings. She was losing control of her own heart, a feeling she resented and yet found thrilling at the same time.

Downstairs Jackson saw that Jim Adams was outside. He said good night to Autumn. Once he walked to the door, he found himself stopping. He looked up at the ceiling. Realizing that his ex-wife's bedroom was just above him. He spoke silently to her. It appeared he was speaking to himself. "A life without heart is not a life worth living," he said to the ceiling.

Upstairs Tiffany had her knees tucked up under her chin. She had lived so long with an endangered and secluded heart. Her drive and busyness had protected her and now she was feeling restless, weary, and vulnerable. Softly she heard "A life without heart is not a life worth living." She raised her head and looked at her bedroom door and around the room. The whisper was so audible she knew it wasn't her own simple thought. She looked once more around the room. She was still very clearly alone, and the house was still. The words spoke to her heart. There had been a lot of strings she had cut loose. Most of them had to do with Jackson and more importantly love. Her soul was on a runway, and it was about to take flight. Worst or maybe best of all was yet to come. John Lennon said, "Life is what happens while we are busy making other plans." She was realizing she was going to have to let go of those tomorrow plans.

Jackson was already walking to his car when he stopped. He froze looking at Tiffany's car in the driveway. Autumn watched her father as if she could see the wheels of his mind turning. She had become fascinated with her father's actions and way of thinking. He was so unique. He turned and walked back over to her.

"Could you do me a favor and park your mother's car on the street tonight?"

She gave it no thought and agreed. She was being trained to realize that her dad had reasons for everything. No word was misspoken, and every step calculated. He kissed her forehead and he left.

Getting in the back of the car, Jim Adams handed Jackson the sidewalk chalk. Jackson smiled and then suggested they go get a cup of coffee. Jackson had some time to kill.

The following morning Tiffany was up early. She had slept sounder and more restful than she had in years.

It was as if her worries, and fear had been drained out of her thoughts. The noise was gone. She walked into the kitchen. She was on her typical morning auto pilot, beginning her morning rituals.

The kitchen window above the sink had come knocking for her attention. Her car was parked on the street. She never parked on the street. She was immediately annoyed. Thought returned to her mind full of questions. Had Autumn gone for a joy ride? Autumn was old enough to drive, but still only had a learners' permit. Unlike most kids her age, Autumn never really showed any interest in driving. Then she noticed her car keys were not in the bowl that usually housed them. She looked around and saw that they had been tossed on the counter. Autumn must have taken the car, a mystery that would be solved soon enough. However, first Tiffany wanted her car back in her driveway and off the street. She was a woman who liked things to be where they belonged. Her car did not belong on the street. She grabbed the keys and headed outside. Her mind was full of the rebuke her daughter was soon to face. As the door slammed behind her it was loud enough to stir Autumn.

Tiffany stopped dead in her tracks. Suddenly, Autumn was innocent of any wrongdoing. Her beautiful offspring had not snuck out in the middle of the night.

Tiffany's heart filled with wonder and her eyes started to water. Written in her driveway with sidewalk chalk was a message that read "Tiffany Riggs, you are lovely. A life without heart is not a life worth living." It was a simple statement made in a broad gesture. It was original, romantic, and sweet. Her feelings in this moment were unlike anything she had ever felt. Briefly she looked around to see if any of the neighbors were seeing this spectacle of love. She was speechless.

    Upstairs a sleepy Autumn was watching and smiling down on her mother.

Chapter 16

The following day Rosemary and Jim joined Jackson in a conference room of Jeff Kenline's offices. The room felt still as they reviewed every tiny detail of the contracts. The acquisition seemed solid. Kenline sat with a few of his own attorneys. All the deeds and documents had covered every tiny detail. Jackson threw a file on the table. He looked at Kenline. "I must ask you. You didn't want this deal, but you took it. Why?"

Kenline explained the character of Barry Jenkins to Jackson as if this were new to him. Barry could be one's best friend or worst enemy. If you were his foe on any level in any arena, he would stop at nothing to attack you. He would destroy your reputation by any means necessary. Kenline had been a sober alcoholic for thirty years, but Barry was making it falsely known he had fallen off the wagon. Nobody was a match for the dirty antics of Barry Jenkins. Kenline was nauseous with worry. Barry had power, influence, and money. A bulldog of a man when he wanted something. In this case he wanted the properties owned by Kenline to turn into casinos. Once Barry had successfully created doubt, distrust, and suspicion among stockholders, he was able to make offers on their stock. He was low balling buying the stock at between 15 and 22 dollars a share. A fraction of its worth. Barry then managed to convince Kenline that the takeover could be hostile or not. Kenline was bullied. He had the option of lawsuits, but Barry had a reputation of bankrupting competitors in litigation. Jackson was at a loss. The agreement may have been wrong in principle, but it was solid as a contract.

Then Rosemary said, "It fascinates me that beachfront property never actually mentions the beach." It was an observation spoken out loud, but not intended for purpose. Jackson lit up; this was an uplift to a cynical situation. Among every tiny detail, the legal description left out the beach. Kenline still owned and had all rights to the beach. Jackson had Kenline's attorneys review the contracts as he watched. Slowly everyone was seeing what they had missed. The beach was not in the contract. It was hard to imagine. Maybe it was supposed to be understood that the beach was included, but none the less the beach was not in the agreement. The beach was not mentioned one single time. Kenline had his ace in the hole.

"This is what you will do. He needs those beaches if he wants those properties. Ask for 15 million per beach on all three of your properties. That will be a 45-million-dollar cost to Barry." Jackson was laying out the plan. Naturally Kenline wondered if this detail would save his hotels.

There were no assurances. Jackson was anxious too, but he didn't wear it the way the others did. Jackson knew Barry would not want to pay. The extra money would be an admission of loss for Barry Jenkins. It was simply unacceptable for Barry to be publicly outwitted. The new light of details was brittle with creative cross-purpose.

As the men talked strategy and Rosemary observed, a surprise came to the conference room's big glass window. Tiffany stood there in tattered jeans and a worn older light green sweater. Her hair indicated she had just rolled out of bed, but she had been up for hours.

Jackson was focused on their recent revelation. He did not see Tiffany staring at him. Rosemary got his attention. When he laid eyes on Tiffany it was as if everything had gone into slow motion. All the voices in the room, though busy, fell silent on his ears. He noticed she was breathing hard. Had she run up the stairs? Was there an emergency? Where was Autumn? His rapid-fire thoughts bombarded his mind.

He walked to the door and stepped out of the conference room. He walked slowly and carefully. They stood looking at each other. Tiffany was still breathing hard. Jackson felt lost. What was his move to be? What should he say?

"You are breathtaking," he offered.

"Shut your mouth," she said with panic and determination. The staring standoff returned. Their eyes locked on each other.

Inside the conference room all eyes were on Jackson and Tiffany. You would never have known they had just discovered the beach loophole.

Jackson's heart was beating almost out of his chest. He had no idea what Tiffany was thinking, her look was intense. She never said a word. All the sudden she ran into his arms. The two embraced more passionately than lovers do. They held onto each other and not a word was spoken.

Jeff Kenline was the first to stand and start clapping. The others in the room quickly followed his example. The healing had begun. All Tiffany could do was surrender to her love of the man she once so fiercely hated. In the embrace it felt like chaos, but there was peace. Something was happening and words would not do it justice. It was not just their love that had been restored, the wonder and joy of it had returned as well. Their love was larger than life. Jackson had won back his bride. He took her hand and led her out of the building.

Jeff Kenline looked back at his two attorneys. "Gentleman, I don't want you to breathe a word about the beaches until we are in the conference room with Jenkins. We will pull this rabbit out of the hat at just the right

moment. In the meantime, you heard the man. We want 15 million per beach and this is non-negotiable." Even Jim Adams and Rosemary Appleman were nodding in agreement.
Cue The Squeeze song, "Hourglass".

Chapter 17

Outside Jackson and Tiffany had just been walking. As they walked Jackson said hello and knew several of the homeless people by name. Tiffany was once again surprised, but not by his behavior. An older version of Jackson would never make time for people that had nothing to offer him. They had managed to walk several blocks down Hillsborough Street and ended up at the clock tower of North Carolina State University. Most of their walk they silently held hands enjoying each other. They seemed to understand each other beyond words and conversation. They walked as lovers at peace with nothing to prove. The courtship was over, and the relationship was rekindled. Tiffany had simply dove in. God had restored her heart. She felt alive.

Tiffany had lived with a division of her heart and head for so long. Her broken relationship with Jackson had deadened her heart. Now she was no longer living with two separate parts of a heart. Every time she looked at him, she felt she could just melt. Jackson stopped walking. The university campus was rich with history, filled with the color of red clay bricks all around them. More importantly, it made for a beautiful back drop to the beginning of their love story. With one of her hands already firmly placed in his, he took her other hand and pulled her into him. They looked at each other with the most intense passion they ever felt. "I love you," Tiffany said softly.

"I love you in this life and the next," Jackson replied. She could feel his conviction. They stood there looking at each other as if they were silently preparing to love each other forever. He then released her hands. She let her grip go as well. He placed his hands softly on her face and pulled her into a deep long kiss. In that moment there was no longing, no ugliness, no hurt. It was the kiss of a sacred romance.

When he pulled away, he led her to a tree in the middle of a wide-open space. He sat on the ground and pulled her gently down to him.

"Tell me," he began to ask. "Where was our first date?" She smiled. This was a memory of her former husband that wasn't ugly.

"Cape Hatteras. We spent the day at the beach and then you took me to the light house. Apparently, you overheard me tell someone I had never seen a real light house. Then when you proposed you took me back to the light house. We climbed the stairs to the top. It was in the middle of summer. I don't think you realized how hot it would be in there. Yet, when we got to the top, both of us were dripping in sweat. You got down on bended knee and asked me to marry you. I had no idea you were going to do that, but I also didn't hesitate. I said yes with great expectation."

Jackson just looked at her and listened adoringly. He thought for a minute. He was thinking hard. He pulled out his phone and called for Jim Adams to come pick them up. He then called Autumn and told her that he and her mother were going out tonight and would be home very late. Autumn was thrilled that her parents were spending time together. She tripped over her words reassuring her father that she would be fine. Tiffany was lost. What did Jackson have up his sleeve this time? She was still trying to wrap her head around the fact that he seemed to know so many homeless people by name. His motives had to be pure because at no point did he brag about the things he did. Was he working with a homeless shelter? Was he simply walking the streets meeting people? The latter seemed most likely to Tiffany.

 Jackson jumped to his feet and offered Tiffany his hand. He was a gentleman in every sense of the word. They walked to the clock tower. Jackson offered no indication of what he was thinking or doing. Tiffany who normally did not like surprises of any nature was throwing caution to the wind. At times she thought to herself that she didn't know who she was around Jackson. She was not a woman prone to surrender on any level or way.

Jim Adams pulled up. Jackson opened the passenger door for Tiffany. He then walked over and told Jim he would drive this time. Jim had never known Jackson to drive ever. Both the old and new Jackson were usually conducting some type of business during rides. Jim hopped in the backseat and Jackson took him to his car. Jim was excited for Jackson because of Tiffany. With a new Jackson, a new Tiffany emerged as well.

With Jim given the night off, it was just the two of them left in the car. "I would ask you what you are planning, but I have a feeling you wouldn't tell me," Tiffany said smiling. Jackson simply smiled and drove. It wasn't long before they were outside the city limits. Leaving Raleigh really piqued her interest. About thirty minutes later they were in Rocky Mount, N.C. "Are you hungry?" Jackson asked. Tiffany assured him she was starving.

Jackson pulled off US Highway 64 into the parking lot of Smithfield's BBQ. Eastern Carolina BBQ is a rite of passage to people in North Carolina. Tiffany eyes were full of flirtation. She hadn't known Jackson to eat at a place like this for years. The old Jackson did everything very high class. She mentioned to him how unusual this was for him to be eating among common middle-class folks. Tiffany was being playful, and Jackson offered her a knowing glance. There was no reason to expound on his past. Though he had no memory of his former self he still had a very good understanding. She was no longer scorched by the fire of her memories.

Cue the Bruce Hornsby song, "Every Little Kiss."

Most of the meal was silent. Jackson had so much he wanted to say, but words didn't yet feel appropriate. He burned with desire to tell Tiffany how much he loved her, but a plan was in motion, and it would have to wait a few more hours. In the past the silence would have been unnerving to Tiffany. However, now she felt at peace with it. More importantly, she felt loved. She felt her entire being was loved. She felt loved for who she was and not what she had to give.

Inside the restaurant at a booth, they were waiting for their BBQ to be delivered. "Tell me about my parents," Jackson asked very unexpectedly. Tiffany was caught off guard. She hadn't expected a question of this magnitude. A grim reminder that Jackson was a man without a past. A magnificent nudge that this new Jackson made her forget about the man he was.

"Well, to be honest, when we met you never talked about your family at all. I just assumed you didn't have any. Since you never talked about them or even made mention of a family, I figured it must have been a painful story. One day, just a few months after we were married, you were on the phone in the living room. I slowly realized you were talking to your mother. I was shocked. I never understood the dynamic there and you never really offered any back story. However, you always held your hand close to your chest. I think you thought opening up was a sign of weakness." She paused as if searching her soul, memory, and wisdom. What should she share? What might hurt the new Jackson? She felt protective of him.

A cute little teenage employee named Destiny brought their food over. Tiffany couldn't help but feel relieved that the interruption was buying her some time to think. Still Jackson's inquisitive look was locked on her. She thought some more and decided he deserved the truth. "I went with you to both of your parent's funerals. Each time you showed virtually no emotion, no tears and strangest of all you didn't offer any condolence to the other family members including your four brothers and one sister. They all cried at some point, but you never did. Your sister Beth once said to me that your silence was deafening. All your other siblings could be read like an open book. You could see on their faces despair, joy, happiness, or sorrow. Not you... no one could ever read your face." Jackson listened and it seemed so unreal to him. He now felt things so deeply. Sometimes he had a hard time deciphering his own feelings from those of other people. The new Jackson picked up on other people's pain, joy, sorrow, or happiness. He could rejoice or grieve with another like most people would never know.

They finished their sandwiches. The vinegar-based BBQ made for some sloppy eating. They laughed at each other like kids in the school cafeteria. Tiffany was still a little perplexed by Jackson. She could see her story disturbed him, but he quickly shook it off and was living in the moment and not the past.

"How do you do that?" She asked.

"Do what?"

"I can tell that learning about your past is upsetting. For once in my life, I feel like I can read your face, but you seem to get over it so quickly. Most people get stuck in a funk over the simplest things. Not you. Not this new you. It all washes right off your back."

Jackson took a deep breath as the stoic side of him came back. "I want to know my history, but at the same time no one is living in the past with me. So why spend too much time back there?" His logic was alarmingly simple but couldn't be more profound, she thought. She asked him once more where they were going. Once again, he simply offered a confident glance and grin.

Back in the car and on Hwy 64 East the drive was peaceful. They enjoyed being with each other. Everything was different from before, but also familiar. It was nice, Tiffany felt. Loving Jackson before had been like driving on a dead-end street. Now on the open road all she could see in front of her was wide open spaces that represented endless possibilities.

She opened the glove box and found a small book of CDs. She flipped through the selection. When she came across The Essential Bruce Springsteen collection, she smiled. Springsteen was their first concert. They couldn't afford seats, so they sat on a blanket in the nosebleed section of an outdoor arena. She slid the CD into the disk player, turned the volume up and sang along to Thunder Road, Born to Run, Rosalita and many more. If she was going to be his shot gun rider it was her job to make sure the music was good. Jackson loved her fun demeanor. He was more than content, he was happy.

Tiffany then played a hidden track from the Born in The USA CD.

"You know most people don't have CDs anymore?" she laughed. "But you were always one for nostalgia. She played a track called *No Surrender*.

"This was always your favorite Springsteen song."

Jackson turned the music up and hit the gas.

Before long they were at the Outer Banks of North Carolina. Suddenly it occurred to Tiffany that he was taking her to Cape Hatteras. Excitement crept into her. She was fully in the moment. Jackson was being romantic. Her wide-eyed gaze paid attention to all the roadside signs. When they entered the small coastal town of Buxton, she remembered their last visit all too well. Jackson parked the car. He looked at her and gave her a tiny kiss on her forehead before he opened the door.

The Cape Hatteras lighthouse is one of North Carolina's biggest attractions with an average of 175,000 visitors every year. Yet today it was not at all crowded. Jackson took Tiffany's hand and led her inside. He insisted Tiffany go first up the 257 steps and he followed close behind. It was hotter inside than he had imagined it would be. Once they were at the top of the 150 feet structure, both were dripping wet with sweat. The concrete building provided no breeze as they climbed the steps. Tiffany found this to be very romantic in one sense, but she also knew that Jackson had no memory of their last visit there.

He faced her. Another prolonged silence. His gaze was fixed on her. She could see the emotion on his face. He looked vulnerable. Then his lips parted in slow motion and words began to flow.

"I don't know much about me. I know I have been a tough and hard man. I know I have been harsh to get things done. I certainly was a man who was willing to engage in a fight or three. I know I have been a foolish and proud man. With the accident I was certainly a broken man. I suppose along the way I have even been a loved man at times." He stopped and took a deep breath. Every word needed to reflect the importance and sincerity he was trying to convey. "It is funny, I don't remember what I was like as a young man. I am not even sure how I won you back in the day. What I do know… what I am sure of… is that I want to give you everything that I am now. The only fight I want in me is to fight for you, us. I want to be your man." He kneeled. His hands empty, he took one of Tiffany's. "I want to be your husband. I want to be the man you always deserved. I can't fix our past, but I can offer you my future if you will take it."

She was never a woman who could be easily hypnotized by usual charms. She had always wanted to be a part of a love that was so much bigger than her imagination. After being married to the old Jackson she stopped searching for anything that made her feel alive. Now she felt as if she was living for the first time in years. Her heart and arms were open. She tried to speak, but words were caught in her throat. She fought successfully not to let the flood gates of tears flow. She simply smiled and nodded yes. "Of course," she said. Jackson was looking at her. He was clearly uncertain of what she would say but was loving the outcome. He rose to his feet, and she almost jumped into his arms. The former lovers, friends and husband and wife were reconciled. She wasn't just in love; she was trusting and most of all felt safe. He didn't simply make her forget other men; he made her forget her former self. The evening sun began singing around them. In motion pictures this time is called the magic hour, the last hour before the sun sets. He looked into her crystal blue eyes. Even The Maldives located in the Indian Ocean could not compare with what he was seeing now. Jackson with his ease, sense of humor, exuberance, and princely smile was the man she loved before they ever met.

Chapter 18

Barry Jenkins fancied himself the grand chess player, a mastermind. He knew he wasn't trusted, but he also knew people feared him. This was something that Barry drew a lot of joy from. He knew he was disliked, but he felt he was more of the author of everything around him. He reasoned that most people never really give the author much thought. His every victory was a beautiful prize. Furthermore, he exercised all jurisdiction over chance.

However, today Barry's anger would be ignited as it had not been for years. He was accustomed to winning. Losing was never an option or even a thought. In the past if he came up against a wall or needed to force things with a strong and intimidating arm, he had Jackson. Barry had always been so impressed with how cunning Jackson could be. He was a man with a huge ego, and he would never allow himself to lose. Barry never had to follow up with Jackson. Even when a matter dragged on for months, he knew Jackson was still at work and never questioned anything. Years of their relationship had been very rewarding for both men. Yet, the new Jackson could hardly be trusted. Barry had no interest in collaboration or mutual benefit, just dominance. Now he was anxious.

Barry slammed both fists on the conference room table. He was surrounded by Jeff Kenline and attorneys from both sides. Kenline played his hand well. He asked for 15 million for each of the three beach properties. Every fiber of Barry's being was on fire with rage. He had been outwitted by Kenline and his attorneys. Barry's own attorneys had tried to argue that the beaches were included in the contracts. The beaches were to be understood. However, the details of the contract clearly made no mention of anything other than the hotels. The details were not made clear, and beachfront had fallen to the wayside. Barry's attorneys dreaded and feared his wrath. Of course, Barry leveled the room with obscenities. Barry would not accept that mistakes had been made. This was his way to avoid blame.

The anger grew. He had no idea or thought of Jackson's involvement. What angered Barry the most was that he knew he couldn't call on Jackson to fix this glitch. Both Kenline and Jenkins knew that this was far from over. Barry would see to it that he tied up this deal in litigation until he broke Kenline...broke both his spirit and his finances. The forty-five million dollars were hardly a concern in terms of Barry's capacity to afford it. However, Kenline was calling checkmate. This was unacceptable.

Barry stormed out of the conference room. As he charged down the hall, he knew he wanted Jackson. Not this new version, but the old one he could count on. His wish didn't take long to realize. Jackson was sitting in one of the leather-bound chairs looking out over the city. Barry was taken back. How dare Jackson have the audacity to be in his office alone. Barry's pace slowed down. He realized that Jackson knew what had just happened and for the first time he suspected or rather knew Jackson helped Kenline.

"You think you are invulnerable but let me assure you there are ways to get even with you," he snarled.

Jackson looked at Barry connecting their eyes. Jackson looked deep into Barry. There was a pause between the two men.

"Who taught you how to be this way?" Jackson asked softly.

The tone and manner of which Jackson spoke spooked Barry, he felt exposed. He tried to be angry, but it was as if he couldn't be. An unrelenting peace was covering Barry. His very soul was defying him.

"I know you hated your stepfather Don. He was never able to understand you and you felt misunderstood your whole life. You resented your father for leaving." Jackson once again paused. He had become good at allowing time for words to sink in and change a person's demeanor. Barry had a slight tremble in his hands. The man had never shared anything personal about his upbringing with the old or new Jackson. Even Barry's own wife and family knew very little about his life and childhood. His youth was that of silent suffering, as his mother had forced a new father into his life. It had given Barry a void that he struggled with for his entire life; a suffering that no one was aware of and now Jackson was speaking to his wounds. Barry wanted to lash out, scream, fight and even hit Jackson, but he couldn't. He felt almost paralyzed to hear his inner thoughts spoken out loud by another human being.

"Your father did leave and that was wrong of him, but he didn't want to, and he did love you. Your mother married your stepfather, and she made it her mission to replace your father. She wanted him gone. She was trying to create a life that wasn't even realistic. Your father did fight for the first five years of your life, but he grew tired from the pain of it all. Your mother used you as a weapon to hurt him. She was very successful. What she didn't see was how successful she was at hurting you. Then with your real father out of the picture, she was able to paint any picture of him she wanted. Though she was wrong she didn't really lie. She believed the things she told you. All the lies were a result of her very mixed-up understanding and desperation to make a family of her own. What she didn't see was that you, her, and your father were still a family, just a broken one." Jackson gave another long pause before he continued. "I know those memories hold on to you like pages from a book you were never supposed to read."

Barry felt a strong pressing on his chest. He hated Jackson even more for speaking these truths. He had hated his father for years and who was Jackson to try and take that hate away. Jackson was wanting to break those chains that bind, but it was all Barry knew. He made his way to the chair across from Jackson. Jackson's eyes followed him. Once seated Barry initiated eye contact.
"Who are you?" Barry asked almost in desperation.
Now it was Jackson's turn to feel stumped. "I don't really know," he answered. This time the pause took hold of Jackson.

He had broken down Barry's defenses. A move that left him somewhat resentful. Now it was time to ask Barry some questions about his own story. Jackson locked his gaze on Barry.
"Why was I in Orlando?"
The question sent shock waves through Barry. How was he supposed to answer this question? Barry thought long

and hard. Jackson never diverted his gaze or attention. He knew his intensity was all the pressure he needed to apply for an answer.

"Henry James," Barry confessed. "He had a mid-size church down there. It was thriving. I am told it was one of the fastest growing churches in America. I don't know too much about church or church growth so who knows."

His answer was more confusing to Jackson. Why would Barry have an issue or even business with a pastor? None of this made any sense. Jackson grimaced and returned his fixed gaze on Barry.

"Her name was Diane Whitaker. She owned the property near his church. It was an old RC Cola plant. The property sits right along I-4. An interstate that runs through central Florida. I had made Whitaker countless offers for the land, but she wouldn't budge. To add insult to injury, when she died, she willed the land to Henry James and his church."

"Ah! Let me guess, the land was prime real estate and you had to have it?"

Barry shook his head yes.

"What did I do to that man?" Jackson asked with disgust.

Barry turned hard. "You don't understand how things worked between us. We had an understanding so to speak. I never asked you about your business, methods, or anything for that matter. It was very "The Godfather" of you. You just always got the desired result that I paid you for. Not one time in all the years did you fail."

Jackson felt like someone had punched him in the gut. He hated who he had been. He couldn't even imagine what he had done to that pastor. Did he use violence, blackmail, or make him some twisted offer that compromised the man and his ministry?

"Did we get the RC Cola property?"

"You didn't have a chance. You left his driveway, and your car was hit. That is when you ended up in the coma."

Jackson was still in disbelief. "He is a good man, isn't he?"

Barry smirked, "By your standards these days I am sure he is, but I wanted that land. He could plant his church anywhere."

Jackson got up and walked to the door. He turned one final time to face Barry. "Life is meant to be shared. You have made a world where you just take and dominate. You are your own prison. I would love to tell you what to do, but you already know those answers deep inside yourself. Take care Barry Jenkins."

Jackson walked out. Barry sunk a little further into his chair. He was angry, but for once in his life he knew his anger was wrong and misguided.

On the other side of the door Jackson pulled out his cell phone. He first called Rosemary. He asked her to book him a flight to Orlando as soon as possible. He wanted to be there tonight. He also asked that she arrange a driver and car to meet him at the airport. Rosemary joyfully agreed and assured him that none of these things would be a problem.

His next call was to Tiffany. He explained he was making an impromptu trip to Orlando after just learning why he had gone there in the first place. He had to know what harm he caused this man, Henry James. More importantly he needed to make amends. He couldn't explain this deep seeded need to correct this wrong above all others. Tiffany was enthusiastic, supportive, and loving. Her voice was upbeat. Jackson thought to himself, *this is how a woman can always be a girl, but a girl can never be a woman.*

"The simple truth of the matter," he said in closing, "is that I have no real idea where this trip is going to take me." Jackson was starting to feel heavy, but the peace that surpassed his understanding came rushing over him once again. They shared "I love you" as lovers often do. Tiffany had only felt a selfishness from Jackson in the past. A relationship that was full of closed systems and structure. Now she was knowing a generous openness. She was excited to be in love again and thrilled to share her life. She was even entertaining the idea of another child.

Chapter 19

Jackson arrived at the Orlando International airport in mid-afternoon. His visit would most likely be quick and, as a result, didn't even bring a change of clothes. Going down the escalator, he spotted his driver holding a sign with his name on it right away. Jackson was very pleasant to the man.

"Do you know..." Before Jackson could finish the driver interrupted.

"Sir, Rosemary made your initial itinerary very clear to me. I know the address and we can be at the home of Mr. Henry James in about thirty minutes. I can't promise the man is home, but we are on the way." Jackson was impressed with both Rosemary and this driver.

They left the airport and took only major highways to the James' home. They pulled into a community called Elder Ridge. It was a lovely little neighborhood most likely built in the early fifties. The smaller houses along the streets were older. However, young professionals were buying those homes and tearing them down to build their own two- and three-story dream homes. Jackson loved that the homes had character, unlike the cookie-cutter stucco homes so commonly seen in Florida.

They pulled into the driveway. Jackson didn't even consider that this was the very spot of his accident. An accident that changed his and so many other people's lives. He explained to the driver that he had no idea how long this visit might last. He could be rejected quickly or could be there for hours. He could not see into the situation as he could with so many people. Once again, he wished he knew exactly what was behind the big front door. He didn't even have a clue what Henry James looked like. Was he an older or younger man? Jackson got out of the car and stood in front of the house for a minute. He looked around surveying the neighborhood. The James' home was a two-story wood frame structure. Most likely one of the very first homes that were rebuilt in the neighborhood.

He laughed at himself for a second. He realized he was stalling, but he also understood this visit was significant. Since he had regained consciousness, he knew he had to return here. He had that feeling even before he knew why or where it was in Orlando he had been. Maybe it was closure of some kind, he thought. Somehow and someway, Henry James represented freedom. Then he walked to the door and rang the bell. Every step felt as if it were happening in slow motion.

Henry James opened the front door rather quickly. As a pastor, he was accustomed to members of his congregation dropping by, unplanned visits that he and his wife Evelyn welcomed gladly. They were all about loving people. Still Henry stood silent when he saw Jackson. The men just looked at each other. Henry was an older man with glasses and white hair. Jackson noticed that he was very much in shape for a man his age. Jackson finally broke the silence.

"Are you Henry James?"

"Yes, and I know exactly who you are," Henry replied. The silence resumed until Henry stepped aside, a gesture indicating he was welcome to come inside. Jackson followed Henry into the kitchen. The men took seats at the kitchen table. Jackson had no idea that he was sitting in the same seat as his last visit.

"I want to start by saying that whoever you think I am, I am not that person."

"I know," offered Henry. "I have heard some stories about you. Although that hardly makes it easy to have you back in my home." Henry offered a forced smile. Jackson found it odd that the man seemed so at ease.

"Can you tell me about my last visit here?" Jackson asked. As the words were spoken Jackson felt that this was the last question that needed to be answered about his old self.

"You wanted me to sell the RC Cola property to the man you work for, Barry Jenkins. I had received some very generous offers from your boss but had always declined. You somehow managed to dig up some dirt on me. Truthfully, it was very impressive that you were able to uncover my past with such precise ease."

"I realize this might be crossing a line, but can you tell me what it was? How was I using this against you?"

"It was almost twenty years ago. Maybe more, I am not too sure. I had been counseling a couple. However, we weren't progressing. The husband had already decided he was leaving his wife. Once that gets stuck in a person's head it is hard to turn it around. Anyway, I kept seeing the woman once and sometimes twice a week. Gradually feelings developed and we had a small affair. It was mostly an emotional thing, but it got a little physical too. You told me you would out me if I didn't sell."

Jackson shook his head in disbelief. What kind of cruel dictator was he trying to be as his former self?

"You were going to expose my secret to my congregation and more importantly my wife. So, of course, I was devastated and even worse trapped."

"There was a child?" Jackson stated sincerely.

Henry sighed, "Yes."

"I am sorry."

"Don't be. After your accident I told my congregation of my indiscretion. It just may have been the most terrifying day of my life. A few people left the church, but not very many. Their forgiveness and support were overwhelming. I had never felt so loved in all my years of ministry and even relationships. In a crazy and maybe even perverted way you gave me that, Mr. Riggs. The Bible does talk about what the devil meant for evil, God uses for good. In fact, our church is now bigger than I ever dreamed."

"And how did your wife handle it?"

"She still doesn't know. At least I think she doesn't. It is hard to tell these days. You see Evelyn has Alzheimer's. I never really had a chance to tell her, but I would have. It was so freeing to get out from under the years of guilt and shame. You see, you set me free."

A happy ending Jackson thought. He felt a little confused. Why did he have such a strong feeling that he needed to come to Orlando? His assumption was to make amends with Henry James, his family and very possibly his church, but none of this was needed.

"Tell me, Mr. Riggs. What can I do for you?" Henry asked with the sincerest smile Jackson had ever seen. Jackson thought hard about the question. He studied Henry James' face. There was really nothing he needed from Henry, but he wanted to need something from him. Jackson felt that he could learn a lot from this pastor. He thought some more and smiled at Henry.

"I think you have already given me everything I needed, Mr. Henry James. I never thought that this would be the outcome of today's visit. Yet, I find your bravery so inspiring. I find your character to be something I hope I can model mine after. Thank you."

Jackson stood up and extended his hand. The men shook hands and then Henry hugged Jackson. There was nothing left to say. Both men wanted to speak, but they both felt instinctively that they didn't want to taint anything that had just happened with unnecessary words. Henry followed Jackson to the door. As Jackson stepped outside, he looked up and the sky was an unbelievable blue. He felt at peace. Jackson thought of Tiffany's eyes at the lighthouse. It was a good day to be so fully alive. Jackson felt accomplished. He felt he had made the amends he needed to make. The circle felt complete.

He walked to his car. The driver had been patiently waiting. Jackson was deep in thought, but the happiest he had ever felt. He had proved his love to his wife and fixed some wrongs. He had become a father to his daughter. He had confronted Barry Jenkins even if it wasn't on his own terms. He felt he knew everything he needed to know about his past.

The driver could sense Jackson's emotion. Again, he was patient.

"Take me to the airport please," Jackson said.

As the Black Lincoln Town car backed out of the driveway, Jackson looked to his right. The truck was coming fast. Jackson started to panic at the impending doom. However, a split second before impact, peace blanketed Jackson one last time. He was dead on impact. No one else was hurt in the accident. Jackson was gone.

Chapter 20

Cue the Ed Sheeran song, "Supermarket Flowers."

Rosemary Appleman walked into Barry Jenkins' office unannounced. Jenkins had one of his Matrix-looking men with him. The intrusion immediately caused alarm and annoyance. Jenkins' secretary followed her in. The secretary spoke before Jenkins could rebuke either one of them.

"I think you will want to hear what she has to say." Then the secretary left the office and closed the door behind. Barry gave the Matrix guy a look and he left. Barry then fixed his undivided attention on Rosemary. She looked to the ground, a timid gesture that was very unlike her, Barry thought.

"He is dead," she said just above a whisper.

Barry stood up. "Who is dead?"

"Passenger side impact. His car was hit by a moving van. He died instantly." She explained but couldn't bring herself to say his name. Oddly, this gave her the strength to relay her message.

She turned and walked out of the office. She would never really be able to recall how she felt during this day in Jenkins' office. She had just shown courage that she would never understand.

Barry was in complete shock. There had been a few times he had wished Jackson was dead, but that was before their last talk in his office. The day that Jackson spoke to his heart. The day that began a shift in the person Barry Jenkins wanted to be. The day he began to realize that the fire that drove his dominance and vengeance did not burn clean.

Rosemary's next visit was to Tiffany and Autumn's home. Jim Adams drove her. The car ride was empty with silence. Happily ever after had come and gone.

Jim Adams waited in the car as was his custom. Rosemary walked slowly up the driveway. Tiffany saw her pull up from the kitchen window. As Rosemary walked, she saw the sidewalk chalk in the driveway that read, "Tiffany, You Are Lovely." The chalk had bled a little from the morning dew, but it was still very visibly clear enough to read. As she admired Jackson's gesture as Tiffany walked out to meet her. Tiffany was in a good and sweet mood, but when their eyes met, she froze. She just knew why Rosemary was there. Tiffany trembled and just started shaking her head no.

"God has taken him home."

Once again words had no value. Rosemary simply hugged Tiffany as she began to weep. Tiffany's deep soul intimacy that had just been born was now dead too soon. In the past the best she could wish for from Jackson was not to be one of his projects. She had finally become his desire and it was met with an ending. She stayed in Rosemary's arms for some time, the tears violently covering her face. In the car, Jim Adams couldn't even watch or look at the two women.

When Tiffany eventually pulled away she said, "He had just learned to live a life fully loved." It was the only thing she felt and the only words she could utter.

Every pew was filled at St. Marks United Methodist Church on Six Forks Road in Raleigh. Everyone from Barry Jenkins and Jeff Kenline to several homeless people had come to Jackson's funeral. The casket was closed because of the impact of the accident. Even Tiffany refused to see his disfigured body. She did not want that to be her final image of her late husband.

Tiffany and Rosemary shared their stories about the Jackson they had come to know recently. Both women were very moving when they spoke. Tiffany walked off the stage. The pastor began to walk to the podium. However, the most unexpected event took place. A very timid and vulnerable Autumn Riggs stood up from her front row pew and walked to the podium. You could have heard a pin drop among all those people in the sanctuary. Even the people who did not know Autumn instinctively knew she was Jackson's daughter.

She took a moment. She gazed at the people, looking into their eyes and faces. Many she knew and many she did not. She found her father's turn out very pleasing. Before she spoke, she thought about how her dad was always good at letting his words sink in, allowing a person to absorb what he was trying to share. She felt like her dad and a smile crept onto her face. Tiffany watched her daughter. She was fixated on Autumn. It was not her daughter's tendency to draw attention to herself in any way.

Autumn's lips parted and words flowed seamlessly. To the average person she was a confident speaker. "Olive Wendell Holmes said, 'Many people die with their music still in them. Why is this so? Too often, it is because they are always getting ready to live. Before they know it, time runs out.'" It astonished Tiffany that her baby girl was speaking without the benefit of any written notes. She had not dared to ask Autumn to share on this difficult and painful day.

"In the days after my dad's passing, I ran across a book by a hospice nurse. Her name is Bronnie Ware, and the book is called *The Top 5 Regrets of the Dying*. Number one is they wished they had lived a life true to themselves, not the life others expected of them. Number two was they wished they hadn't worked so hard. Number three was they wished they had the courage to express their feelings. Number three really struck a chord with me. Number four was they wished they had stayed in touch with friends. And the last number five was they wished they had been happier."

She was modeling her father once again, allowing her words to settle on the hearts of the people in front of her. It was during Autumn's break that Rosemary looked over at Tiffany, a mother that was simply in awe of her daughter's words and courage.

"My dad has left us and that is so not the plan I would have made. Yet (she paused) I know for certain in the final months of his life, my father lived a life that was completely void of Bronnie Ware's Top 5 regrets. So, to all of us I say, let his strength give us strength. Let my father's faith give us faith. Let my dad's hope give us hope. And above all, let my daddy's love give us all love."

As the tears streamed down Tiffany's face, she didn't even try to conceal or wipe them away. She was her daughter's audience. When Autumn stepped away from the podium she looked out across the crowd. She took another moment, but this one was not for her words to sink in. This time it was a moment for herself, one for her to see the faces of the people her father had touched. She saw tears in the eyes of the homeless few that attended the service. She saw Barry Jenkins' head bowed. She wondered if he was hurting or ashamed or both. She tried to read every face gathered before her. In that moment she didn't just love her father, she wanted to be like him. *How far they had come since his accident,* she thought.

A few days later, Jeff Kenline was in his office when a relaxed Barry Jenkins arrived. Kenline's secretary ushered Barry in. Barry placed a small stack of paperwork on his desk. Kenline immediately saw a different Barry Jenkins. The two just looked at each other...Kenline curious and Barry ready to make amends. The death of Jackson Riggs changed who he wanted to be. Barry nodded and laid all the contracts and hotel ownership papers in front of Kenline. "Sometimes it takes death to give us a freedom we never knew our story needed or could even have." Barry left.

In Orlando Florida, Henry James walked to his mailbox. There were two unidentified envelopes. He opened them. One was a healthy check for his church. The other envelope contained a substantial personal check made out to him with a note that simply said, "For you and your family. Amends."

Cue the James Taylor song, "Shower the People."

Made in the USA
Columbia, SC
05 April 2023